The Story of Pooville

Fenton Roades

THE STORY OF POOVILLE

iUniverse books may be ordered through booksellers or by contacting:

iUniverse
1663 Liberty Drive
Bloomington, IN 47403
www.iuniverse.com
844-349-9409

Because of the dynamic nature of the internet, any web addresses or links
contained in this book may have changed since publication and may
no longer be valid. The views expressed in this work are solely those
of the author and do not necessarily reflect the views of the publisher,
and the publisher hereby disclaims any responsibility for them.

Any people depicted in stock imagery provided by Getty Images are
models, and such images are being used for illustrative purposes only.
Certain stock imagery © Getty Images.

ISBN: 978-1-5320-8784-4 (sc)
ISBN: 978-1-5320-8783-7 (e)

Library of Congress Control Number: 2020910107

Print information available on the last page.

iUniverse rev. date: 07/17/2020

This book is dedicated to my wife,
but please do not tell her.

Contents

Chapter

I

Meet the Poos

George Poo was born in Manchester, England, in 1860. He was born into a middle-class family and was the oldest child of Henry and Mildred Poo. George was the most curious of the Poos and was always trying new things as a lad. He grew up and received a college education and became a schoolteacher at the Wilson School in Manchester. He was responsible for teaching all forms of science to the ninth-, tenth-, and eleventh-grade students at Wilson School. George Poo was known as a good teacher who always presented new ideas to his students. Oftentimes, his students won awards for new and innovative ideas. Professor Poo, as he was called, often received awards for his teaching skills.

He was by far the most successful of the Poo family. He had four brothers and three sisters, all of whose accomplishments fell short of George Poo's, although George's father, Henry Poo, and his twin brother, Pepe Poo, were very successful in the horse-manure-hauling business. While he was going to school, young George worked part-time in his father's business, shoveling poo. He liked shoveling poo but wished he could figure out a way to do something profitable with all that poo rather than paying to dispose of it in the dump.

Throughout the mid-1800s and into the early 1900s, the elder Poo brothers dominated the horse-manure-hauling business. As Henry Poo always said, the Poos were meant for that business—and they were. Pepe Poo always said, "I love the smell of horse poo in the morning, or in the afternoon, or even in the evening," and Henry always agreed.

"I never met a horse I didn't like," said Henry Poo. "It's the smell of money." They always lamented, "If only we could find something to do with all this poo, we would be rich," but they never could figure out what to do with the poo, except to dump it in a landfill, which cost them money.

But all in all, they made a good living. At the peak of their business, they had more than thirty wagons hauling poo. The company was sold in 1910. The automobile did the company in over the next thirty years, but during Poo's time, the Poo brothers were raking it in and were well respected in the field of poo hauling and horse manure.

George's younger four brothers were not as motivated as George. Thomas, who they called Tom Poo, got a job shoeing horses at the public stables in downtown Manchester. His father, being influential in the poo-hauling business, helped Tom Poo get his job. Poor Tom never seemed to have any luck. He was kicked in the head while shoeing a horse at age twenty-one and killed instantly. The Poo family was devastated.

William, who they called Billy Poo, and his brother Peter Poo, who was nicknamed Pete Poo, both worked in the local ink factory. There is not much known about these Poos, but it was thought that they did a pretty good job making ink. We do know that they both married and had little Poos. How many Poos they had is not documented, but the speculation was that they had a lot of little ones running around. Wallace Poo was the youngest, a lazy fellow who seldom had a job. Wally Poo, as he was called, died of the flu at a young age. There is not much known about him.

George's three sisters were quite another story. These were triplets who did everything together. Penelope Poo, who they called—you guessed it— Penny Poo, together with her other sisters Patrice

Poo, who they called Patty Poo, and Margret Poo, who was called Maggie Poo, all lived together in Manchester. Together they started the Poo Family Laundry. These Poos were quite successful in the laundry business. None of the three ever got married. These three Poos always stuck together. They all lived long lives. None of them left Manchester, and they all died within a year of one another. It was thought that those Poos died in their seventies, but official death records for some reason are not available.

George Poo married Martha McCarthy of London in May 1893. George was thirty-three, and it looked like this was one Poo who was ready to settle down. He was now quite established at Wilson School as a capable teacher. Martha was a pretty girl who was born to be a mother and homemaker. She had a good heart and wanted to make George Poo and the Poo family as happy as she could. She also wanted a lot of little Poos to raise. It wasn't long before George and Martha had their first Poo. It was a boy they named Paul. They immediately nicknamed him Pauly Poo. They thought it was catchy. More Poos came along pretty quickly. Peggy Poo was the next to arrive. You guessed it. They nicknamed her Peg Poo—a big girl with a great laugh and a good sense of humor. Twins ran in the Poo family, and George and Martha had two sets of twins back-to-back. One set of identical boy twins and then a set of fraternal twins, a girl and a boy. That was a lot of Poos.

The twin boys were pretty perky Poos, full of life. They were named Peter Poo after George's brother and George Jr. The other set of twins were named Pepe Poo after Henry's brother and Betsy Poo after Martha's sister. The family was really coming along. Things were stable over the next ten years, and the Poos were busy raising their family.

Chapter

II

The Poos Move to America

Around the turn of the century, the Poo family was in generally good spirits. George Poo was elevated to the head of the science department at the Wilson School. He also applied for and received several patents involving the use of fertilizers and started to receive several small royalty checks annually for their use. This was one of George's favorite fields of study, and he was quite knowledgeable on this subject. Around this time, George and Martha Poo purchased a modest but very nice house not far from the Wilson School. The house had only three bedrooms and two bathrooms, but it had a large backyard for the kids.

George had a substantial tuition discount at the

school because of his position as science head, and he enrolled each of the Poo children in Wilson as they became of age to go to school. Betsy, who they called Bettie Poo, passed away in 1899 of an infection from a cut she got on her leg. The family was very upset, but infections were big killers in those days because of the lack of antibiotics. Outside of that unfortunate happening, all in all, the rest of the Poos were doing just fine.

Over the next ten years, the Poos raised their family, educated their children, and did all the things that an English family did in those times. England was expanding its empire and was one of the most powerful countries in the world. George, who had worked at the school for many years, was growing restless to try something new. He knew he had a large family to raise and a lot of mouths to feed. In a lot of ways, he was discouraged by the politics in England, especially in Manchester. The Liberal party was growing quickly. The Poos were starting to feel threatened. He heard a lot about what was going on in America, a place of great opportunity where people were free to do what they wanted. There were many people who left England to try to find a better life in America.

Over the next year, George and Martha discussed the possibility of moving to America. George had some savings, and the house had been paid for and could be sold for a nice profit. They also had a nice severance package from the Wilson School. He had been there more than twenty years. They felt that the combination of those three things would provide enough money to get them established in America. They made the decision to try their luck in America.

In June 1909, immediately after the school year ended, the Poos were off to America. There were quite a few ships going back and forth between England and America at that time. The Poo family scheduled their crossing and arrived with their possessions in the port of New York in August 1909. They were welcomed by immigration. They were just what America was looking for to help build and educate the nation.

After being processed through immigration and spending a few weeks sorting things out and seeing New York, the Poos decided to go to Philadelphia. Philly was called the City of Brotherly Love and lived up to its name. It was a hodgepodge of different nationalities. South Philly was mostly Italian; north and northeast Philly were mostly Polish, Irish, and English; and the area west of the city was called Germantown. It was part of Philly but predominantly German, with some English. That was where the Poos decided to settle.

They purchased a house in Germantown for

half the price of what they sold their old house for in Manchester. By Manchester standards, it was a small mansion—five bedrooms and three bathrooms sitting on almost half an acre of property. That much space was unheard of in Manchester for the average middle-class family, but America was just getting started. There was plenty of cheap land available. The Poo family loved their new home.

George Poo applied for a position with Quaker Chemical Company as the head of research and development. He was hired. They were headquartered in downtown Philadelphia and had a large facility fronting the Delaware River. This was necessary for a convenient way to ship finished goods and receive raw materials. The Delaware was a great way to move products to other locations— the preferred and cheapest method at the time. Quaker Chemical Company eventually became Quaker Oil Corporation, one of the big players in the oil business for quite a while in the US.

Martha Poo went about raising the children and being a stay-at-home mother. Things were going pretty well, and the Poos were able to hire a part-time maid to help around the house. George Poo was very successful in his new position. He patented quite a few new products for Quaker and made some very good investments. He received stock options, which he exercised, and within several years, he had made several huge profits. He also purchased a large tract of land not far from Philadelphia, to the northeast. As luck would have it, Philly developed right into his land, and he sold it for an enormous profit. George never shared what he made on this transaction, but it was rumored to be over a million US dollars, a huge sum for that time.

Chapter

III

George's Big Idea

George Poo and his family of Poos had prospered beyond their wildest dreams. Moving to America was the best idea George Poo ever had. He lived in a fine house and drove a 1910 four-door Oldsmobile sedan Deluxe, one of the finest cars available. By all measures, George was a very successful man, but he was restless. He was always thinking about his father's manure business and the possibilities if he could harness the power of the manure to make fertilizer. One of the main problems he saw was that the horse population was rapidly declining as the automobile gained in popularity. George knew that horse manure was rich in the nutrients he needed to make his fertilizer but felt that, in the future, if he relied on horses to get the necessary manure he needed to make fertilizer, the price would be continually going up because the supply of horses would be continually going down. He was probably right. Realizing that the horse population was on a serious decline was the major reason for not using horses' manure for the base material for his fertilizer. He had managed to come up with a way to eliminate the bad side effects and increase the effectiveness. It was a true breakthrough.

George had been experimenting for quite a long time in his spare time with a new method of making fertilizer. His experiments told him that he had hit on a method to make fertilizer that was almost too good to be true. His test results showed that his new method produced a fertilizer that increased crop output by over 50 percent without any side effects. Some crops showed a 75 percent increase in yield. Because he did not believe his findings, he repeated his experiment at least twenty times over a period of three years. In every test, his results were off the charts. Each new test was better than the last. He knew he had hit on something big, but he was not sure how to go about making it happen. This was a radically new idea. How could he get folks to give up their poo? You see, George was experimenting with human poo—a very personal situation.

In the past, in a number of countries, human poo had been used to fertilize fields to grow various crops—night soil, as it was called. In many cases, it produced poor results because the human poo was used in its more natural form. This introduced various diseases into the crops being grown. There were cases of sickness being spread through the population that ate food that had been grown using night soil. George solved this problem by developing a revolutionary way of processing human poo by combining it with other nutrients and refining the human poo using a high-heat boiling technique. He was convinced that his fertilizer could change the world for the better.

George had a Poo family meeting and spelled out the entire situation with his invention. After much consideration and discussion, everyone agreed. Martha and the Poo children, who were getting older and starting to enjoy their own lives, reluctantly agreed with the plan. For this idea to work, George felt that he would need to start a new town where he could bring his idea to reality with some degree of privacy. He needed to control the quality of the poo that he was using in his fertilizer. The only way he could do that was to control what people ate. You see, as mentioned, George was experimenting with human poo. He discovered that humans made the best poo for making fertilizer if you controlled what they ate and combined it with his methods of production. Controlling the donor's diet was the key to making great fertilizer with human poo. George knew this was a new concept, one that would require some delicate introduction into American and worldwide society. He also realized that he would need to make the idea of supplying human poo to his fertilizing plant one that would reward the poo donor. He was on a very slippery poo sloop. If he did not do this correctly, his idea would be forever gone. What to do?

Chapter

IV

The Town of Pooville is Born

It was 1919. George Poo had just turned fifty-nine years old. The first World War had just ended. Most of Europe had been affected by the war. There was a severe lack of food throughout Europe. The United States was taking an active role in providing as much of the shortfall as possible.

George was still full of energy and was up to what he felt would be a monumental task but a great step forward for humankind if he could pull it off. Because of the devastation caused by World War I, among other things, the world was in desperate need of more food, and George was bound and determined to help provide it.

George wanted to make his new company a family affair. He wanted to assign his wife, Martha, and his five children specific responsibilities. He felt that if he built his company with Poos in key positions, it would strengthen his control over his operation. Martha had always been a stay-at-home mom. She was used to running the house, and there she would remain. All the Poos were still living at home, so her role would remain the same as always.

Pauly Poo was attending La Salle College in Philadelphia, majoring in business and accounting. George earmarked Pauly to eventually run the financial side of the business, which was exactly what Pauly Poo did. Peg Poo oversaw everything related to food. That included ordering, prep, cooking, delivery, and more. It was going to be a huge undertaking, and she needed a large group of helpers to pull it off. George referred to them as dooers.

George Jr. and Pete Poo oversaw manufacturing the new fertilizer that the company was going to make, a very tall order considering they were starting from scratch and nothing like this had ever been tried before. Pepe Poo oversaw growing all crops and buying and maintaining all the livestock. Again, he was starting from scratch to put it all together. George Poo Sr. was going to be the driving force in this new endeavor and would guide his family in putting their operations together.

George's first step was to find a piece of property

that was sufficiently secluded so that he would not be interfered with but would be close enough to people populations to get the necessary poo donors. He found what he thought was the perfect piece of land in southern Maryland. It was more than 320 acres and had frontage on the St. Clemens Bay and the St. Clemens River. George felt that these natural barriers would help shield what he planned to do. Being able to control what he was about to do without interference was an important part of George's plan. There were also major pockets of potential poo donors in Baltimore, as well as in smaller cities and towns in and around the area. Those areas were booming. George purchased that piece of property and immediately incorporated and created the town of Pooville.

Housing was in demand back in Philadelphia, so the Poos had no problem selling their house for a nice profit. George and Martha Poo and the family took up residence in several of the existing structures on the property that George had purchased.

George wanted to build Pooville out in a specific way to allow for an efficient method to control and harvest poo. Poo was the main ingredient in his new fertilizer and the only ingredient he could not buy on the open market. He had to get large quantities of human poo under controlled conditions. It was a tall order to say the least.

George hired a group of approximately fifty construction workers and supervised the first phase of the Pooville build-out. He decided to make phase one, as George called it, entirely out of wood because there was plenty available, and it was the least expensive building material. He was not sure if his concept would work, and he figured he would build larger, more permanent quarters after he got the bugs out.

Phase one consisted of clearing and leveling approximately forty acres of his parcel. He started with what he called a *pooatorium*. It was a building two hundred feet long by fifty feet wide. It had a walkway constructed around one length and both sides. A series of doors were installed. Each one led to a two-foot-by-three-foot room containing a hole with a seat over it. There was a vent at the top of the door. These were installed on three sides of the building. The back was open. There were 150 of these little rooms installed in his first pooatorium. On the inside of the pooatorium was a continuous shelf, one foot wide, which ran below the holes. Metal buckets were placed under the holes to receive the poo. It was a fairly simple process, but poo had to be processed quickly, or it would lose some of its effectiveness. George was not sure how long he had to process the poo once it was deposited, but it was high on his list of things to determine. George felt that one pooatorium would be enough to start collecting and processing poo.

In addition to the construction of the pooatorium, George had a crew busy making twenty buildings for housing poo donors. The units were built for sleeping only. Nothing else. George did not want these units to be comfortable. He was interested in his donors doing two things: eating and pooing. Each building had four separate units elevated a foot off the ground. Each unit was twelve feet by twelve feet and contained four bunks. Each bunk was elevated so that you could place your belongings under your bunk. All in all, they were tight quarters. There were vents that ran along the top of the buildings for ventilation, and in one corner was a small coal heater to keep the pooers warm in the winter months. George started out with the ability to house 320 pooers. Each building was numbered so that George could keep track of where each pooer was housed. He felt that was the minimum number of pooers required to supply the poo he would need to meet the initial demand for his fertilizer.

Also under construction was a cafeteria. This building was open and airy. It had lots of windows and was brightly painted. There were many tables that sat four pooers each. There were also some other bigger tables that held up to twelve pooers.

On one long side of the building was a counter that ran the length of it. Behind that was a full, open kitchen containing many stoves, ovens, a prep table, and storage cabinets. It was one of the largest cafeteria facilities ever constructed and was very inviting. It was also made so that the food cooking could be smelled throughout the cafeteria. Attached to this building on one side was a lounge with sofas, comfortable chairs, and a bookcase well stocked with books, games, and more. There were also snacks everywhere you looked. On the other side, there were banks of showers equipped with everything necessary to have a nice, relaxing experience. Clean clothes and daily showers were also provided to all pooers and were required daily. Each pooer was given a number for identification, similar to a social security number.

Chapter

V

Does Anybody Want to Poo?

Geoge had a vision of what he wanted for the town of Pooville. He was looking to create both a company and a town that would provide a total experience for all of its inhabitants. George also wanted to create a place that would take someone from the cradle to the grave, a place that provided for its inhabitants in every way. This was a radical new idea, a tall order for George to deliver, but he was determined to try. If he was successful, it would be a very special place indeed and one that could be controlled by him and the Poo family.

At the front entrance to Pooville, George erected a large sign with the words *Town of Pooville* on it. Underneath, it read *Established 1920*. There was a ten-foot wood privacy fence that ran along the front and sides of the cleared property, with guarded gates at the entrance. A simple look, but it supplied the security and privacy that George Poo was looking for.

George knew there were many serious issues that needed to be solved. For Pooville fertilizer to be made to optimum strength, he needed to supply a very high grade of both meat and vegetables in order to get the highest-quality poo. He planned on growing everything himself, but until that was possible, he needed to depend on the local farmers for his supplies of livestock and vegetables. George put his twin boys, George Jr. and Pete Poo, who were now in their twenties, in charge of getting the necessary food and assuring its quality. They came through with flying colors. Peg Poo, who oversaw food prep, cooking, and storage, spent countless hours putting her operation together and preparing for what was about to happen. All the Poos took their roles very seriously. They pulled together as a family unit.

George also worried about getting donors. He was not sure that anyone would want to come to Pooville for the purpose of giving him their poo. This had never been tried before on the scale that George figured he would need to make it work. George decided to make some signs and post them in several of the towns that were not too far from his town and see if anyone showed up. He got six three-foot-by-five-foot poster boards and neatly put the following ad on them:

ATTENTION
The town of Pooville is looking for donors.
Food and lodging included. No work or
skills required. Apply at entrance. Weekdays
between 8:00 a.m. and 5:00 p.m. Must be
over sixteen years old. Everybody welcome.

George posted three signs each in two towns close to each other and within walking distance to Pooville. As he was coming home, he had a sinking feeling that this would not work. Why would anyone show up for his job? He didn't want to tell them that they were donating their poo. He figured they would think he was a kook and that would scare them off. He posted his signs late Friday afternoon so that a lot of folks would read them on the weekend. He had a meeting with his family and his staff of twelve. He was hoping a few donors would show up so he could get started.

Chapter

VI

Long Live the Pooers

G eorge and his entire family and staff were running around all weekend trying to get things organized. His construction crews were busy trying to finish all the details that they had overlooked in their building. They told George that he should have given them another week to finish, but George said, "If I did, then next week you would come to me again, asking for another week. We have to try this thing sometime. Now is as good a time as any."

Early on Monday morning, George and his family were woken up by a lot of noise on the side road. It sounded like a caravan coming down the road. It was still dark, maybe 5:30 a.m. George was thinking, *That can't be folks coming for my job.*

He threw his clothes on and headed to the front entrance. His house was a mile or more from the entrance, so it took him a little time to get there. Sure enough, there were at least two hundred folks crowded together at the front entrance, ready to become donors. George was beside himself. *Now that they are here, how do I convince them to become poo donors?*

He told his greeters, "Once you have them signed in, we will assemble in the cafeteria for a talk on what this is all about." George said to cut it off at about two hundred people in the first round. That was about the capacity of the cafeteria.

The first group in the cafeteria was very mixed. George and his whole family were astonished at the potential donors. There were young and middle-age Whites, a few Blacks and Asians, some old and young ladies. George prepared to address what was basically a cross section of the entire society. The potential donors were anxiously waiting for George to tell them what this opportunity was all about.

George peered through the curtain for a few minutes, looking at his potential donors. He was gathering his thoughts. George was thinking about the importance of what was about to take place. He started to wonder if this was a one-time event—or did he discover something about people in general? Peg was sitting next to George. They were both numb. George pulled back the curtain, wondering if the folks would embrace what he was about to tell them or if they would call him names and walk out. George had no idea what reaction he would get, but he was about to find out.

George called Peg over before he went in front of the people and asked her to run down to the entrance and see how many more were signed up to be donors. He asked her to be quick because his pitch would be based on what she told him.

The Poos served some goodies to the crowd, and he had a couple of fellows who were in the contractor crew but were good musicians play some country songs while he waited. Everyone seemed happy and did not mind waiting. They seemed excited that someone cared about them. Peg returned and told him there were about eight hundred signed up, and more were coming down the road.

George said to himself, *Hey, you only have 320 spots right now. You need folks who can poo. The more they poo, the more valuable they are. I need pooers.* At that moment, he decided to eliminate the old ladies and the old men. *Good folks, I'm sure, but not good pooers.* He figured that if most of them stayed after he told them what he was up to, he would try to focus on the big, fat men and women. If a donor could poo twice a day or three times a day, he or she would do the work of three donors—a valuable donor.

He wondered if he could get any three-a-day pooers. *Is that possible?* All these crazy ideas were going through George's head. He needed poo. He needed it now. This was his shot at getting the best pooers. George came out of the back room and introduced himself.

"Good morning, and thank you for coming. I am excited to share with you today what we are doing here in Pooville. My name is George Poo. I am a scientist and the founder of Pooville. My wife, Martha, and my six children live here in Pooville, as well as many others who are helping me to build the dream that I have for you and for Pooville.

"I have invented a new revolutionary form of fertilizer that will raise crop yields from 50 to 75 percent over the fertilizers that are being made today. I have not found any fruit or vegetable that I have tried my formula on that has not at least doubled the yield. This invention is truly revolutionary and will help people all over the world have more food to eat and live a better life. I need your help to make this happen because my miracle fertilizer is based upon using human waste. I need your poo in order to make my fertilizer." George then stopped to see what would happen. For a few seconds, there was silence. Then he could hear some laughing, and then people started shouting.

"Where do I sign up? Where do I sign up?"

Chapter

VII

Shut Up and Poo

George immediately understood that asking for poo was not going to be an obstacle. Of the first session of two hundred applicants, George signed up eighty. When the next two hundred came in, he gave the same talk and got the same result. Almost everyone wanted to sign up. He accepted only forty applicants. It took two days to fill all 320 beds.

He figured once he got rolling, the demand might require as many as two to three thousand pooers. If only he knew that down the road, he would need to house an army of pooers to meet his demand. He had his construction crew continue to expand the sleeping buildings. He also started construction on another bigger pooatorium and another cafeteria, more elaborate than the first one. George wanted his pooers to stay in the cafeteria all day, socializing, eating, pooing, socializing, eating, pooing, and so on. Every pooer had a number. George had trackers at the pooatoriums keeping a tally on how many times a day each pooer pooed. He knew that he had many potentially good pooers available. When he saw that a pooer was only capable of making one poo a day, he replaced them with a new pooer.

George also changed the way he introduced new potential pooers to his company. Instead of trying to sell them on his idea, he told potential applicants how lucky they would be to join his army of pooers. The applicants bought in hook, line, and sinker. Pooers started to gain status as an important part of the company. George started a public relations campaign via signs and newspaper articles, touting the wonderful life that the pooers lived. The word spread of this job opportunity, as George called it. The number of applicants increased daily.

George now had thousands of applicants to choose from. He developed a profile of the perfect pooer—sex, race, height, weight range, age, personality. He gave a simple personality test to determine if they would be happy and content spending their life pooing. Over the next year or two, George created a pooing machine. He found that the perfect pooer was generally big. They were at least forty years old and single. A big frame and being slightly overweight was ideal. Height did not seem to matter very much. The laid-back type was much better than the go-getter. Introverted or extroverted personalities did not seem to matter. George had the perfect profile for a great pooer figured out. It was referred to as the PPP—the perfect pooer profile.

George got rid of the poor pooers, replacing them with those who met the pooer profile. After he did that, the contentment level of the pooing community got much better. There was very little conflict. Most of the pooers were happy eating and pooing and being taken care of by the town of Pooville and the Pooville company.

The makeup of the Pooville pooers was about 60 percent men and 40 percent women. There were no children in the pooer community. Men and women were housed in separate sleeping buildings. George discouraged men and woman pooers from getting together, having romantic relationships, or having sex. He did not want to deal with women getting pregnant. If a woman got pregnant, George immediately terminated her services and replaced her with a new pooer. There were no exceptions to that rule, and females were told of the rule when they were hired and signed a statement stating that they understood the consequences of their actions.

Although George did not realize how the pooers would react to pooing for a living, several things started to become abundantly clear. The vast majority of pooers were content never leaving Pooville. The main topic of conversation was usually food. "What is going to be our next meal?" This was everyone's favorite topic of conversation. There was nothing stopping them from taking a weekend off, but seldom did any of them ask for time off, even though there was no actual pay for pooing on weekends or any other time for that matter. George constructed a very nice visitor center near the front entrance for pooers to meet friends and family. George did not want any visitors snooping around in Pooville. However, very few pooers had visitors or even asked if they could have visitors. The day of the week did not seem to matter. They enjoyed the pooing community and eating, pooing, and repeating the cycle.

This was a very content group of folks. Being taken care of by Pooville was what they were interested in having done for them. Having housing, food, clothes, and so on was why they bought into this program. That seemed to be all they were interested in. Their lives were fulfilled.

Chapter

VIII

The Pooville Company Is Born

George was far along with perfecting his fertilizer formula. He had set up a pretty efficient way of accumulating and moving poo through the various stages to make it fertilizer. He had many obstacles to overcome in order to make his product with the potency that he promised. His research lab made some great progress in ramping up his production to more than sixty burlap bags containing fifty pounds of Pooville Miracle Fertilizer each hour. George had a warehouse containing several thousand bags of fertilizer ready to sell. He also figured out how to stabilize the potency of his product after it was manufactured. He was ready to start advertising his fertilizer.

Pooville was in a farming community, so George figured he would try to get some of the farmers interested in trying his fertilizer. He got his foreman in charge of distribution and told him to get the biggest wagon they had and fill it with bags of fertilizer. His timing corresponded with the planting season that was about to happen. Over the next month, he visited every farmer within a fifty-mile radius and gave each farmer a fifty-pound bag of fertilizer.

At the time, all farmers were using some type of fertilizer on their fields. There were a few popular ones out there. Some were better on some crops than others. It just depended on what you were planting. George did not care about what the farmer was planting. His fertilizer worked on every crop and could be distributed over a much larger area in the field. Pooville's fertilizer had higher yields on some crops than others, but all yields were at least 50 percent higher than the yields of his competition. He told each farmer how to use it, and they had to promise to isolate his fertilized area from the others. He asked some of the closer farmers if he could visit during the growing season to see progress. They all agreed to let Pooville monitor crop growth.

After he completed the fertilizer giveaway, he hired a sales/marketing team to sell his product in a five-state area. The year was 1921, and George had spent a good portion of his savings. He knew he needed to ramp up sales, or he would run out of money. He was also in the middle of a Pooville building boom and did not want to slow down progress. He had assembled a very motivated group of employees and did not want to have to lay off any of them. He employed more than two thousand people. He went to several local banks in the area, but they laughed him out of the bank. That didn't bother George one little bit. He believed in what he was doing. He called them the little people and moved on.

George hired and trained ten traveling salesmen, single men in their twenties. He knew they would be away from home most of the year. They all had at least a high school education. A few had some college. He preferred kids that had grown up on farms. Locals were the best, he thought. He got each one of them a pickup truck, filled it with fertilizer, and sent them to different areas over a six-state area, including Pennsylvania, New Jersey, New York, Delaware, Virginia, and Maryland. These were primarily commissioned salesmen but with a small monthly draw.

Within the first three months, Pooville Fertilizer Company was shipping three hundred bags of Pooville Miracle Fertilizer per day. Within six months, they increased that to a thousand bags per day. George had to pull his sales force back to Pooville for a break so that he could get caught up on production and shipping. His salesman made a 2 percent commission on every bag of fertilizer they sold. They were getting rich and loving it, and so was George. They were begging him to let them go back in the field, but George told them that they needed more training. He put them to work for a month in the research lab, really getting to know the product they were selling. These guys loved George, as his entire company did. George loved to give those who wanted to better their lives the opportunity to do just that. On the other side of the coin, he also wanted to give the folks who wanted to do nothing with their lives the opportunity to do just that, providing him with the resources to make the dooers very successful and wealthy at their expense. He was loved equally by both the pooers—the poo donors who elected to eat, sleep, and poo their lives away—and the dooers, who were also helping George and the entire Poo family. Both groups were helping George and the Poo family become very rich and successful.

George and his family did their best to keep the pooers isolated from the dooers. Each group knew and saw the others, but it was just small talk or a greeting. Socially and economically, these two groups were separate in every way. There were never gatherings where the two groups interacted. Whenever there was a celebration like Christmas, the Fourth of July, or other holidays, there were always separate celebrations. They had nothing in common except the mutual goal of manufacturing and selling Pooville Miracle Fertilizer. For the pooers, they knew but really did not ever discuss that subject. They were more interested in the menu than anything else, and George, the family, and the dooers were very happy with that. The dooers were interested in obtaining wealth and the trappings that went along with it, but there was no animosity between the pooers and the dooers. Each group was happy in their own environment.

Chapter

IX

Smells Like Money to Me

*A*bout a year had passed since George started selling his Pooville Miracle Fertilizer, and the new growing season for most crops was about to begin again. The news of this new product spread by word of mouth throughout the American farming community. There were so many farms that had tried the new fertilizer in the last growing season that reported fantastic results to their fellow farmers. Now, almost every farmer in the country, with a few exceptions, wanted to plant at least part of their fields using this new product. Many farmers were all in and wanted nothing else for their fields.

To say that George Poo and his entire company were overwhelmed with the orders coming in would be an understatement. At his current production rate, it would take more than two years to fill the orders he had received in the last month. George did not want to lose any customers, and the last thing he needed was his sales force going out to try and drum up more business.

George was a smart fellow who really thought problems through. This was a good problem to have, but he had to distribute the product he had in stock and the product he could produce in time for the growing season in a fair way—a way that would show fairness to both the large growers and the small farmers alike. What to do?

George asked for and received hard numbers on inventory and total expected production for the next several months. He figured, based on the data, he could supply about 20 percent of the total orders to his customers in time for the growing season coming up. He assembled his sales force and told them to fill their pickup trucks with product. They were itching to get back in the field and start making more money. George sent them all in different directions with a list of the farmers who had placed orders for his product and the quantity that they ordered.

He told his salesmen what to say to each farmer so that they could get different fertilizer for their shortfall from another supplier. He instructed his salesmen to assure each farmer they visited that by the following growing season, Pooville company would be able to supply all their fields with Pooville Miracle Fertilizer. He also told his sales guys that they would still receive their commission on their existing accounts as well as any new accounts they brought into the company.

George knew it was a tall order to meet the demand now and in the future, but he had a year to deliver on his promise. He knew he could get more pooers, which was his biggest obstacle to increasing production. He was processing 100 percent of the poo produced. He would need to at least triple the number of pooers that he currently had. That meant housing, more cafeterias, and other facilities. He decided to increase the sleeping buildings by ten times the current capacity. Each building would house one hundred pooers. He constructed two more much larger cafeterias to provide eating facilities, and he constructed two mammoth pooatoriums. They would allow for the simultaneous pooing of more than five hundred pooers at the same time. Each pooatorium was also a production and processing plant, so it instantly increased production the day it was open for pooers. He also doubled his construction crews to support this new building effort.

George set his plan in motion, and it came

off without a great deal of problems. He did have occasional shortages of lumber and some other materials, but he found new suppliers. He had an extremely loyal and motivated group of employees. They all knew that Pooville's growth and success would translate into additional money and wealth for them. He referred to them as his dooers.

George was an extremely generous employer. The Pooville company margins on fertilizer sales were currently over 60 percent. The company was starting to realize a positive cash flow. George distributed 10 percent of the profits equally for every dooer, regardless of their position. It was equal shares for everyone. The pooers received no money distribution. They did not really need money. Everything was taken care of for them. They really did not care about money. George threw huge gourmet eating parties for them. The pooers were very excited and appreciative whenever he did that. He would have music and hoopla at each event and appear personally to thank them for their loyalty and their great pooing activity. Then he would give them a pep talk about trying to increase their poos per day. The pooers would all shout out a commitment to poo more. The events were a sight to see. This was a group of happy pooers.

George was ramping up phase two of his build-out, but he was starting to face a huge issue with getting enough food—enough good food. Pooville grew vegetables and raised chickens, pigs, cattle, and more themselves. It was impossible for Pooville to grow and raise all the food necessary to feed all these pooers. They were running out of space to grow crops and having other technical issues. Let's just say George decided to head in a new direction. He wanted to raise his own livestock. He needed to control what they ate. Vegetables and other produce were a little different. If the fruits and vegetables he needed were grown using his Pooville Miracle Fertilizer, he was good using them. He had his sales force make a deal with certain farmers to buy a large percentage of some of the crops that they were growing using Pooville Miracle Fertilizer. The farmers were happy to sell their crops at a fixed price before they were grown. The deals took a lot of pressure off the Pooville dooers but still maintained the necessary quality George was looking for in his fruits and vegetables. In most cases, the cost difference was negligible because he sold the fertilizer at full price. It worked out to be almost the same cost.

Chapter

X

Organize the Dooers

*A*nother year passed, and most of the new improvements and capacity spelled out in phase two was completed. Pooville was ready for a banner year, and boy did they get one. Orders poured in at triple the rate of the previous year. George Poo and his Pooville Fertilizer Company figured they would have a pretty popular product with his fertilizer, but this was beyond all his expectations. He had several warehouses filled to the rafters with fifty-pound bags of fertilizer. It all sold within a few weeks. He was cranking it out at a rate of two thousand bags per hour. Every hour. Seven days a week. His margins continued to increase as he continually became more efficient and his volume increased. The cash was really starting to pile up. The neighboring town that had a bank told George that they would open a branch in Pooville just to accommodate his company. The Pooville company was by far the largest employer in the area.

George, now in his sixties but with a lot of things to do before he left this earth, was thinking about the dooers. How could he reward these folks but get more control over them and more work and effort out of them? He felt he still had a lot to do, and he needed to exercise more control over them and reinforce their loyalty to the Pooville company. A lot of the dooers lived here, there, and everywhere. That was all about to change.

George had saved about a fifty-acre parcel of his property that fronted the St. Clemens Bay. This was a spectacular piece of his property that was completely undisturbed. He assembled his department heads, which basically included his children plus about another ten dooers who filled needed top spots in the company. He explained his plan to them. He wanted to get their feedback prior to going to the lower-level dooers with his plan. George's idea was met with a very positive response.

George decided to have a meeting with the dooers and introduce them to his concept of having them all located within the town of Pooville and living in this area. This was mandatory if you wanted to work for the Pooville company. The company would construct all the houses at the company's expense. The company would own the house, but the dooer would have the exclusive right to live there, and they would also be responsible for maintaining it. This would allow every dooer to reside in Pooville as one big happy family. Each dooer would receive a residence that corresponded to their position in the company. The company would build the houses, and it would be part of each dooer's benefit package if they remained working for the Pooville company. If the dooer was promoted, their residence would be changed to reflect their new status. George had a catered affair at the site and cleared just enough of the land so that all the dooers could see St. Clemens Bay and the beautiful surroundings. After that meeting, George could do no wrong. The site was beautiful. All the dooers were on board.

George constructed a series of buildings containing very nice apartments for the lower-level dooers. They were extremely happy with the accommodations. George made one-bedroom, two-bedroom, and three-bedroom units depending on family size. Then he developed a half a dozen different sized single-family homes. He mixed the more modest homes together with the nicer ones.

There was no segregation. He wanted the lower-level dooers to mingle with the upper-level dooers. It worked better than George thought. It seemed that the dooers were always working. Even when socializing, they were talking shop. George built a house for him and Martha on the bay but in the middle of everything. He wanted dooers to talk to him. He was very interested in knowing what was going on and the current thinking of the group. There were no fences, walls, or barriers of any kind allowed in the development. The walkways were continuous between houses. This signified the openness of new ideas from one dooer to another. He also created a beautiful clubhouse with a gym, pool, playroom, and more. On the outskirts of the development, he constructed an eighteen-hole championship golf course, and all dooers were automatically given an exclusive membership. Only Poo Company employees and their guests could play on this course. As usual, George shot a hole in one. Everyone was more productive, and George Poo had his dooers right where he wanted them—under his control.

The Pooville company was one of the pioneers in developing the campus method for maintaining the loyalty and longevity of its employee population. Elements of this method have been copied by many companies over the years, especially tech companies.

Chapter

XI

The Expansion of Pooville

*A*t this point, the Pooville company was not selling its miracle fertilizer outside the US, but the company was receiving intense pressure from large, growing operations in Europe to sell to them. The US had a huge price advantage over everyone else in the world for their crops because of their far greater yield advantage. European growers, both big and small, were clamoring for Pooville Miracle Fertilizer. Over several years, the Pooville company bought prime farmland throughout Europe and held it in various shell companies. Pooville company was not working the land but was preparing for Pooville's entry into the European fertilizer market.

Before George introduced his company to

Europe, he wanted to be sure he had enough capacity to provide all US farmers the fertilizer they needed and that he had added the necessary volume to supply the European market. It took several years of expansion for George and his company to accomplish this, but at last he had achieved his target and was ready to start selling his fertilizer to European companies and to start leasing Pooville-owned lands to local farmers, with the promise of providing Pooville Miracle Fertilizer as part of the lease. The land that he paid rock-bottom prices for skyrocketed in price. George was able to get top dollar for his land leases as well as a premium price for his fertilizer. Before he introduced Europe to his fertilizer, he heavily shorted all the existing European fertilizer companies, a move that eventually helped make George one of the few billionaires on the planet. The US was deep in a recession after the stock market crash of 1929. Pooville Fertilizer Company was a privately held company. Besides his shorts, George had no funds tied up in the stock market. Any money he had to invest had been put into his company. George was clearly in control and could do basically whatever he wanted. There was only one entity with the power and no entity with the will to stop him from progressing in any way he desired. The Pooville company was becoming one of the most powerful companies in the US and in the world.

In January 1935, the Pooville Fertilizer Company shipped its first container load of miracle fertilizer to Europe. It was destined for the farmers who had lease agreements with the Pooville Fertilizer Company. The growing season had not started, but he wanted to get his product to leased land farmers first to show them good faith and to let them know that the Pooville Fertilizer Company was good to deal with. The farmers were very pleased with his actions, and it built great loyalty from this group. There were over a thousand leases of farmland in force throughout Europe. This was a large group of elite growers. He then supplied the other small farms throughout Europe with fertilizer, and the largest growers and operators were last. All the European concerns involved received enough product to take advantage of the new growing season, but George wanted the big boys to know who was in charge. Very early on in their long relationship, they realized the reality of their position, and they accepted the Pooville company's actions because they really had no choice.

Pooville's venture into Europe was very profitable and increased Pooville's sales by almost 40 percent. Pooville's profit margins were increasing every year and were now in the 65 to 70 percent range. George and the Pooville company were very pleased with the numbers but felt that they could still squeeze a little more out of the operation through a combination of increased sales and efficiency.

Chapter

XII

Where Have All the Pooers Gone

The Pooville company and the town of Pooville were nearing their twentieth anniversary. The year was 1940. There was a huge celebration planned throughout Pooland, as it was nicknamed by the pooers and dooers. Everyone who resided in the town of Pooville considered themselves very lucky indeed to live in such a beautiful, peaceful place. It was truly considered by all its inhabitants to be the land of milk and honey, where everything was provided for them.

The backlog of those who wanted to become a part of the Pooville experience was huge, especially considering the sad state of the US economy at the time. There were many pooer and dooer applications considered before an offer of employment was made when there was an opening. Turnover was small and not a particularly big problem at the Pooville company, but it did happen. Most departures were related to the situation with the pooers. The Pooville company screened their applicants very closely, but occasionally, one fell through the cracks.

George was very pleased at the way things worked out, but he did have a few nagging issues that were tugging at him for answers. George had hundreds of thousands of pooers who resided in Pooville and supplied poo for the Pooville company's fertilizer. Some of them had pooed for the Pooville company for almost twenty years. Very few ever left once they were given the position. The pooers considered themselves privileged, and few had visitors or left town or the pooers' area.

The pooers were completely segregated from the rest of Pooville. They were given everything that they needed to exist and to live a happy life. They were given no reason to think about anything except eating and pooing. The media outlets available at the time were closely monitored by Pooville. There was no information that was given to the Pooville residents if it was not in Pooville's best interest for them to receive it. You may say that the media was controlled by the elites—in this case, the Poo family and their Pooville organization.

The pooers' area was surrounded by a system of fifty huge cafeterias. Some were set up similar to the fast-food restaurants of today, serving pizza and other popular items on a 24-7 basis. A pooer could eat at these places whenever they wanted, night or day. They never closed. There were twenty-five more of these cafeterias conveniently scattered throughout the pooers' assigned area. The other twenty-five were specialty cafeterias that had staggered openings throughout the day and night. The menus varied, and the pooers could make suggestions for meals. This setup kept the majority of pooers eating all day long. Many pooed four to five times per day and were proud of it. You might say that they were full of poo. Some of the facilities had live entertainment. They were the backbone of the Pooville experience. Everything else revolved around their production. There would be a long line waiting for a cafeteria to open when a popular dish was being served. Eating was the reason for the pooers to exist.

A pooer rarely lived past sixty years old. A lot of them died much younger. At the end of the pooers' days, the majority of them were obese, many in the 350- to 400-pound range. Some needed a wheelchair to get around. The older ones were passing away at an alarming rate, mostly from heart attacks. George and some of the other prominent Poo family members started to question the idea that supplying everything necessary to live was a good idea. Maybe doing the thinking for folks was not such a good idea. "Are we depriving these folks of a long, meaningful life? Should we be giving them the opportunity to do things and to think for themselves?" George and family labored over these issues, debating back and forth. At the end of the day, George concluded, "How else are we going to run this place? If the Pooville company cannot enslave these folks, how would we ever get the poo necessary to make our fertilizer? Our goals have nothing to do with their well-being. This is a socialist order that has been organized for the betterment of the Poo family and the Pooville company. Without the pooers buying in to the whole scheme of what we are doing, we could never be successful. God bless the pooers."

Very few of the pooers' next of kin bothered to come and pick up the pooers' bodies when they passed away. This was after several requests when the Pooville employee services departments attempted to contact the next of kin. The third attempt included a form with a self-addressed stamped envelope that allowed Pooville to dispose of the body how the Pooville company saw fit. It was a total release over what would be done with their remains. Pooville built several huge freezers to accommodate the bodies awaiting the pooers' next of kin to pick them up for their funeral and burial. Prior to being frozen, Pooville would perform a few procedures that were necessary to prepare them for transport but not burial. Boy were they stacking up. They had an in-house doctor on staff to keep everything legal and on the up and up. All paperwork, including death certificates, were completed to the letter of the law.

The other issue really nagging the Poo family was that the Pooville Fertilizer Company was a single-product company. George had filed for and received many patents on his miracle poo fertilizer, but they would be running out sooner rather than later, and competition was sure to come into the picture. George was now almost eighty years old and knew his days were numbered. He kept thinking about the thousands of frozen pooers that he housed in his freezers and how many more were dying all the time. How could he use this situation to his advantage? He asked a small group of his R&D staff to take a few of the frozen pooers and see if they could come up with anything.

George felt that their findings were very encouraging. The dead bodies were rich in nutrients from the good food that the pooers had eaten. With preparation, they could be ground up and mixed with fillers to provide a new product—a granulated mix of ingredients that could be spread on crop fields to increase the crop yield and to nourish the depleted soil. It was just the kind of product the Pooville company needed. The trials went very well, and it was an instant hit when it was introduced. Pooville went into full production on this product and added it to their product line.

The R&D folks also came up with another use for the frozen pooers. Their bodies were usually very big and extremely rich in the nutrients that were given to livestock. The Pooville company introduced a product that, when added to the livestock's normal feed, would add over 20 percent to their weight over their growing period. They could mix it with growth hormone enhancers to make it more effective. The Pooville company R&D department could not believe how well the trials went. George introduced both of Pooville's new products. There was instantly a huge backlog. His profit margins on these new products were in the 70 percent range, and he knew that once they were introduced and ingrained into the farming community, The Pooville company could raise the price rapidly. George called his new products

Pooville's natural miracle field rejuvenator and Pooville's natural miracle animal growth enhancer.

The demand was intense. George had his accounting department start to track the life cycles of his pooers. If Pooville could increase the age of bringing in new pooers by five years and hire heavier pooers, mortality rates would be substantially increased. George and the Pooville company knew that they would have real issues meeting future demand without making changes to their pooing population. They needed to increase mortality rates of the pooers by 10 percent in order to have enough inventory to meet their expected demand for their new products.

Chapter

XIII

Times Marches On

Over the next fifty years, the town of Pooville became one of the wealthiest and one of the most desirable places to live in the entire country. True to its roots, everything in the town of Pooville revolved around the success of the Pooville Fertilizer Company. With the exception of ten huge farms that were purchased in other locations throughout the US to grow crops and support livestock, the town of Pooville remained the one and only location to manufacture the Pooville company products.

George Poo Sr. retired from an active role in the company at eighty-two years of age. He passed away at the age of eighty-eight. An impressive bronze statue was erected in his honor and was placed in the center of town near the entrance to city hall. Pauly Poo, George's oldest son, was groomed to succeed his father when he retired. Pauly became both chief operating officer as well as chairman of the board of directors of the company. Many of the Poo family members held very important positions throughout the company, but because of the size of the company, many important positions were held by other names outside the Poo family.

The town of Pooville and the Pooville Fertilizer Company now occupied a total area of over seventy square miles. In order to keep one of George's favorite slogans alive, "what happens in Pooville stays in Pooville" (I bet you thought Vegas came up with that one), the entire town of Pooville was enclosed either by natural barriers like rivers or with walls with twenty-four-hour security. Coming and going was tightly controlled. Daily reports of the comings and goings of all pooers, dooers, vendors, visitors, and so forth were kept. Security was constantly updated as new technology became available.

During this period, the Pooville company grew their employed dooers to more than two hundred thousand and the pooers to more than one million strong. Also, over this period, the company virtually captured every farm in the US as their customer. The situation throughout the rest of the world was pretty close to the same. There were some countries that the Pooville company decided not to enter because of instability of the government, logistics, or some other economic reason, but for the most part, if the Pooville company invited you to become a customer, you complied. It just made good sense.

The Pooville company supported a few of the remaining fertilizer companies trying to compete with them because some of the committees in the federal government were complaining about the Pooville Fertilizer Company being a monopoly, which of course was true. The company, through their lobbying activities, convinced the committees investigating them that the Pooville company was clearly not a monopoly. It did not take long before the entire investigation was dropped. At this point, company management was able to pull funding from the last few remaining fertilizer companies and complete the intended plan of having complete control over the US and European fertilizer markets.

The Pooville company increased their lobbying activities through the hiring of additional individual lobbyists and lobbying associations. Association with lobbies now became a continuous and permanent part of their operation, but it was a very small percent of their overhead, considering how much benefit the relationship achieved. They pretty much owned the government representatives and could now do pretty much anything they wanted without government interference.

That included pricing their products at whatever price they wanted them to be (I'll bet you thought the drug industry came up with that one) as well as ridiculous fees and nonsense taxes (I'll bet you thought the giant cable company came up with that one) that no one understood, but it had to be paid, or you would be cut off from your supply of fertilizer. Wow. What a concept.

The Pooville company was at the forefront of business in the US and the world as it entered the modern age. The Pooville company was a Fortune 500 company that was well positioned to be a force in the world economy.

Chapter

XIV

The Great Poo Shortage

The year was 2002, and the Pooville company had fully established a multiple product line for their sales and marketing department to advertise. They locked in as many of their customers as possible to the concept of fertilizer and rejuvenator for their fields on a rotating growing season basis. To better plan for their production and to gain customer loyalty, they organized their marketing program so that their products were used in alternate growing seasons. This allowed for much more streamlined manufacture of their products. The system worked very well for them because the Pooville company could now supply half of their customers with fertilizer and the other half with their natural field rejuvenator product. It also allowed their customers to get two years out of their fertilizer instead of one, a big savings for them. Of course, the Pooville company increased the price of their new products to compensate, and it had the effect of increasing profit margins. Cost increase was negligible. The new concept was very successful. The following year, the company would reverse the process. Their natural livestock enhancer was harder to schedule because it was in constant demand. It was a real winner for them. Revenue increased substantially.

The Pooville company was being investigated by several watchdog and activist groups who were testing the Pooville company's products to be sure that the products they produced were safe for human consumption. They were interested in looking at Pooville's products, including their additive for improving livestock growth. The Pooville company always stressed how natural their products were, and that was true to an extent, but there was a lot of chemistry and additives that went into these products that tended to alter nature somewhat. The Pooville company had no intention of sharing any of their findings or research with the public about how these product mutations would affect those who consumed the products grown with the Pooville company's products. Company headquarters was regularly visited by both lobbyists and crooked politicians to assure the Pooville company that the additional funding they were providing prevented any interference with their products. While there were major safety questions and concerns being raised, the government insisted that all the Pooville company's products were safe and effective. It was business as usual for the Pooville company. There were several countries in Europe that banned the Pooville company's products because of safety concerns, but the company denied that they were not safe and said that those European companies had no basis for their findings. It was just a bump in the road for the Pooville company.

Over the last several years, the Pooville company tried to shorten the life cycle of their pooers by hiring older pooers and targeting overweight and generally out-of-shape individuals. The strategy worked even better than they projected, and pooers were dropping like flies. The demand for products produced from dead pooers was increasing at an accelerating rate, and the Pooville company did not want to run out of raw materials for their products. It was working a little too well, and the pooers were starting to notice the alarming rate at which they were passing away. The company assured the pooers that it had nothing to do with their chosen lifestyle, but a lot of the pooers were getting restless about the whole situation. Pockets of pooer protestors were starting to develop. It was a pretty sticky situation for the Pooville company, and the pooers were sticking together on this issue.

This was generally a group of pretty satisfied individuals. They needed to do nothing but eat and poo. The Pooville company had created a pooing machine. There was almost no dissention among the pooers. An occasional issue would develop between two pooers, but it was an isolated situation. This new situation felt different to the Pooville company.

The Pooville company decided to have several gala eating parties. Extra-special food and extra desserts as well as top-notch entertainment were provided. They had one party a week in different locations throughout the pooer area. All this was an effort to smooth things over, calm things down, and get back to eating and pooing as usual. It did not work very well. The protests continued.

There were no cars located in the pooers' area, but there were free shuttles that ran day and night that would take a pooer to any cafeteria or pooatorium they desired. There was some but generally very little green area in the pooers' habitat. It was pretty packed with eating, pooing, and sleeping buildings. There was no room for much else. This was a densely populated town of pooers. There was no money of any kind needed by the pooers. Everything was free. You might say it was a cashless society.

As a protest, a small group of pooers decided that instead of going to the pooatorium to poo, they would poo right where they were when they got the urge to poo. It started on a Wednesday morning in July, and within a week, it had spread to more than 10 percent of the pooer population. There was a lot of poo lying around the pooer area. Besides creating a huge mess, there was poo everywhere and anywhere. Production of Pooville products started to suffer and soon grinded to a halt. The protests were creating a poo shortage in Pooville, and the place was turning into quite a smelly mess. The pooer area had always been immaculately kept. Cleanliness was a hallmark of the Pooville company. They spent a lot to keep the pooers' area free of any disease and to keep them happy. They wanted nothing to interfere with the pooers' routine.

Pooville company management was in panic mode. What could they propose to calm down the pooers and get them back to the business of pooing? The pooing area was turning into a huge toilet. The smell was getting hard to take. The dooers who lived all the way across town were starting to complain about the smell coming from the pooers' area. This was really the first major crisis in Pooville that could not be paid off in some way. Top Pooville company management met all night and into the long hours of the morning to develop a plan that would calm down the pooers. After much thought and deliberation, they felt that they hit on a solution.

Pauly Poo, who was elevated to chief operating officer and chairman of the board of the Pooville company after George Poo Sr. retired, organized a meeting of all the pooers. There were too many pooers to meet in one place, so the company used their huge movie screens that had been installed in all the cafeterias for movie nights, and Pauly Poo addressed the entire pooing population at one time. Of course, a special meal was provided for the pooers to entice all the pooers to attend. The pooers were very interested in attending. They wanted to know what additional free stuff they would be offered to end the protest. There was excitement, and the smell of poo was in the air.

Pauly Poo was cut from the same cloth as his father. He was very well respected and liked by both the pooers and the dooers. His words carried a lot of weight, and he knew it. It was not necessarily what ultimately happened that was important. It was how it was accepted by the pooers that mattered. What was done was not nearly as important as how the whole population of pooers perceived what Pauly Poo said to them.

Pauly addressed the crowd in his usual diplomatic way, assuring the pooers that immediate action was going to be taken to help the life expectancy of the pooers to increase. Pauly was a born politician. He presented a three-pronged health plan to accomplish this goal. First, Pooville was going to establish a series of free health clinics strategically placed throughout the pooers' area. They would provide twenty-four-hour service with doctors and a full nursing staff. Second, as part of this program, each clinic would have a prescription and pain clinic attached to the health clinic to immediately fill any prescribed medication required, and third, any pooer who was prescribed drugs would be monitored electronically and reminded when to take their medication and when to pick up their free refill. Refills could also be delivered directly to them so as not to interfere with their busy eating and pooing schedule.

Pauly then told the crowd that starting immediately, Pooville was going to adopt a green agenda to ensure the health and well-being of all the pooer population. He told them that the Pooville company would spend vast sums of money to put this green agenda in place for the well-being of the pooers. He did not get into the specifics of the plan. The pooers seemed to love the idea. They had no clue what Pauly was talking about, and neither did Pauly Poo, but just the fact that the company was willing to spend a lot of money trying to make things green and better for them was all they needed to know.

The crowd went wild with delight. The Pauly Poo Plan, as it was nicknamed, was accepted hook, line, and sinker. As the crowd was filing out of the cafeterias, they talked about ways they could increase their eating and pooing efforts for the company. They also were questioning how the cost of these initiatives would be paid, but they said, "Hey, it's not our problem how they pay for it. We just eat and poo." It was not long before the poo was cleaned up around the pooers' area, and things got back to normal. Overall, poo production numbers rose by over a percentage point after the meeting.

The result of the health/pill clinics being provided in the pooers' areas was that the life expectancy of the pooers declined, but the pooers were so medicated now that none of them seemed to care. The green initiative was a bunch of signs designating green areas as well as some newly landscaped areas for the pooers. They only provided a few benches because they did not want the pooers to spend much time there. You know, eating and pooing. They also painted all the cafeterias and pooatoriums a very nice shade of green. The pooers loved it. The result for the Pooville company was nothing but positive. This was a small price to pay for this positive of a result. Production of both poo and deceased pooers increased. It was a win-win for the Pooville company. The whole incident strengthened their control over the pooer population, and doing the green thing had been a stroke of genius. The Poo family was becoming very, very rich.

Chapter

XV

Drugging the Pooers

The Pooville company was really humming along. The town of Pooville and the Pooville company were on stage as a world leader. The Pooville company was at the top of the heap in all the important metrics that judged a successful company.

All the supposedly free stuff that was being supplied to the pooers turned out to be a win-win not only for the Pooville company but also for the drug companies involved. The Pooville company, as part of their preparation for the meeting with the pooers, contacted several of the major players in the drug industry to determine how they could help with drug discounts as well as supply and delivery issues. They were told that they were very interested in opening new markets for their products, especially opioids. They were really under the gun from the government to control who they were shipping opioids to. Deaths from opioid drugs were sky rocketing. There were more than 1,300 deaths from opioids occurring every week in the US. The drug companies and drug distributors were advised that heads were going to roll if they did not get the situation under control. It was becoming impossible for politicians to keep looking the other way on the opioid issue. The vooters were also really starting to get up in arms. The poo was about to hit the fan.

The town of Pooville was a pretty isolated place. There was a little but not much information getting out regarding the goings-on in Pooville. This was exactly the kind of situation that the drug companies were looking for. Representatives were sent down from the selected drug companies that were to supply medication to the Pooville clinics. The reps set up the clinics and filled them with all the necessary drugs and other products that they handled free of charge. They said it would be a great way to get them started; just consider the first shipment free samples. The Pooville company appreciated their help with the setup. It was not long before both the health and medication clinics were open to the pooers.

The clinics became very popular places for the pooers to go for an examination between eating and pooing. Usually they showed up at the clinic complaining of an ache or pain. After a thorough examination by the attending doctor, a prescription was sometimes written for medication to help the pooer. It could be filled next door free of charge. How convenient was that for the pooer population. Eventually, lines formed at the clinics for an examination. It got so bad that it started to affect the eating and pooing routine of the pooers, so it was set up that seeing the doctor was by appointment only. Medications were refilled automatically and delivered to the pooers. All pooers now wore monitors, so the company always knew where they were when delivering their prescription. The pooers really appreciated the service. They loved living in the town of Pooville.

The result of the whole setup was amazing for the Pooville company. The pooers were happier than ever before but passing away at a much faster rate. Opioids were having a huge effect on the pooers. Overdoses were very common. It increased the mortality rate by so much that the Pooville company was able to increase their production of both the natural miracle rejuvenator and the natural livestock enhancer by almost 10 percent. This became an important part of the Pooville company strategy. They instructed their lobbyists to spend whatever was necessary to handle any added pressure if it arose. The lobbyists told the Pooville company it would be no problem to handle the situation. They had everything under control.

Pooville, in another stroke of genius, realized that the pooers really had very little if any income. The Pooville company applied for subsidies for them and received enough to almost completely pay for their medications.

The Pooville board asked their engineers to try to figure out a way to develop a more predictable and orderly way to get their supply of inventory for their field rejuvenator and livestock enhancer. In collaboration with another company that specialized in making genetically modified plants and grains, the Pooville company came up with a product that they called PMO. It was genetically programmed into the crops that were grown for the pooers to expire in a more orderly fashion in order to have a steady supply of pooer inventory. A system that through genetic engineering could terminate a pooer's life in an organized manner so as to provide a steady supply of raw materials for their products. This helped the company not need to add new storage facilities. Because pooers had to be frozen at a very low temperature to ensure freshness, these facilities were expensive to build and maintain, and utility costs were high. This new system was very effective in cutting down on the rate of adding new facilities and streamlined the hiring of new pooers.

Chapter

XVI

Let the Best Pooer Win

The town of Pooville together with the Pooville Fertilizer Company sponsored an annual pooing contest. This contest was in its fifty-first year and was the highlight of the year for the pooers' community. The hierarchy within the pooer population was established by being selected by your fellow pooers and then doing well in this contest. It could be compared to our Super Bowl or World Series.

A great number of the pooers in Pooville were given special names by the other pooers. This was a close-knit family. Pooers had very little if anything to worry about. They were completely taken care of financially, socially, medically, and so on. The only real rivalry among the pooers was how much they could poo. There were pooers who could really drop the poo. They were nicked named the Poo Droppers, and many of them were very popular, which is why they were given special names.

The Pooville company sponsored an annual pooing contest that always took place during the summer months and pitted the best pooers against one another, as elected by their peers from each individual housing unit to represent them in a pooing contest. There were more than two hundred pooer housing units in Pooville. That meant that about four hundred pooers were in the pooing contest because two pooers were selected from each dormitory. A lot of great pooers were in the contest. They all had special names. Some wore special T-shirts or hats to signify what housing unit they represented.

The winning pooer received a private room for the following year, starting in January, that had a huge sign over the doorway, letting everyone know that he or she was the Grand Poopa for that year. They were given the official title of the Grand Poopa for the year and a huge trophy. The Grand Poopa also was cleared to have consensual sex as long contraception was used, and the winner received a special embroidered shirt and a special hat to wear for the year that signified him or her as the Grand Poopa. The shirt was embroidered with

Grand Poopa, and the hat had a huge poo affixed to the top of it. The poo looked very real, but it was just a very high-end rubber reproduction. The old Grand Poopa would present the new shirt and hat at the annual ceremony to the new Grand Poopa. Wearing the shirt and hat around during the year was a great honor. The pooers had great respect for the winner of the pooing contest every year. The other pooers always put the Grand Poopa at the head of the line, whether it was for eating or pooing.

To determine the Grand Poopa, there was one scale that determined the weight of the poo. There was one designated place that all candidates pooed in the pooatorium. The total poo for the day was weighed and tallied to determine the winner for the day. The results were posted on a giant poo-o-meter at 12:01 a.m. each morning. The poo-o-meter was round and was over ten feet in diameter. It was located right in the middle of the main green area, which was almost right in the middle of the pooers' area. Each week, 10 percent of the pooers were eliminated based on total weight of the total weekly poos—a very fair system. There were several attempts by contestants to add weight by swallowing lead weights and other heavy objects, but they were always discovered. If a pooer was caught doing this, they were banned from being in the contest for life. This was considered a very serious offense. The scale was calibrated before the start of the pooing contest but could not be recalibrated during the contest to be sure it was fair to all pooers.

The contest went on for a total of ten weeks. The remaining contestants after ten weeks had a poo-off that was decided by seven days of pooing with all the poos being added together. The most weight won. No exceptions. There was a committee of ten that made sure that the contest was on the up and up. Five were from the Pooville company dooers, and five were elected from a vote of the pooers. The committee was elected by secret ballot.

The pooer contestants were in many ways elevated to a high status among the other pooers, especially during the contest. They were given special names like Pooing Papa, Poo Momma, Pooee, Poo bear, Poo Bellem as well as many other nicknames. For the Pooville company, this was a way to give the pooers a distraction from their pretty noneventful lives. The pooers looked forward to the contest every year, and some of the better pooers had a ritual that they went through to get ready to compete in the pooing contest and when they were getting ready to poo. You just can't make this stuff up.

This year's contest was extra exciting because

of the number of famous pooers who were in the contest as well as the addition of many new pooers who were trying to make a name for themselves. As the contest went into the tenth and final week before the playoffs, the excitement was really mounting. You could have heard a pin drop looking up at the poo-o-meter when the playoff-bound pooers were posted.

Pooville company management always booked a famous classic rock band to celebrate the event, and there was a huge party held to celebrate the pooer playoffs event. Going into playoff week, there was heightened activity throughout the pooer area. Many signs, T-shirts, and hats were worn showing a pooer's favorite pooer. Many new pooer names were born. The new pooer stars. Just a few of the new pooers' nicknames were Poo Poo, Poo Girl (four female pooers made the playoffs—a first for the contest), Pooa, Dr. Poo, and Charlie Poo.

There was a total of thirty-six pooers who made the pooer playoffs. During the ten weeks of the contest, three pooers had to drop out for health reasons, and two died from suspected opioid overdoses, but natural causes were listed as the cause of death on their death certificates.

Twice a day, standings were posted on the results of the pooer playoffs. The poo-o-meter posted each name, and nickname if designated, and the total weight of their playoff poo. No weighting was given to their ten-week standing. This was a whole new poo game. Many times, it was only a few ounces that separated one pooer's ranking from the next one. The pressure to poo was unbelievable. The calculations were scrutinized very closely. All weightings were recorded so that results could be reviewed if necessary, in case of a dispute.

The pooers were pulling out all the stops to produce the maximum amount of poo possible, and many had a special eating and pooing ritual. The whole thing was really a sight to see. The competition was intense. As the contest came into its last day, most of the pooers isolated themselves. They ate immense amounts of food and performed many rituals that they felt would help them make more poo. At 11:59 a.m. on Super Poo Sunday, the results were posted. At three o'clock in the afternoon, the new Grand Poopa was crowned in an elaborate ceremony. Almost every pooer in Pooville attended the event, and even many of the dooers attended. Of course, all the Pooville top brass were in attendance. Pauly Poo, the chief executive officer, personally made the presentation. The pooer in second place was also up on the stage for the presentation. They were advised of their responsibilities in the event the winner was not able to serve out their term. They also became an instant celebrity.

After the tightest race in the history of the Pooville company pooing contest, Poo Bear was named Grand Poopa with much pomp and circumstance. This was the first time in Pooville history that the Grand Poopa won back-to-back championships. Pauly Poo announced that a statue of Poo Bear would be erected in his honor. The statue would be installed on a platform beside the poo-o-meter in the designated green area. What an honor.

Poo Bear was beyond words in his acceptance speech. He became the most popular pooer in Pooville.

In second place, trailing by only a few ounces, was Pooee. He was given runner-up honors and was instructed in his responsibilities in the event Poo Bear was not able to perform his duties as Grand Poopa.

Many other pooing celebrities were born as a result of the contest. All the pooers in the pooer playoffs became well known. Many very funny but serious stories were told by the contestants regarding the goings-on behind the scenes to increase their poo productions. The pooer community hung on every word. It was the main topic of conversation for many months after the contest ended.

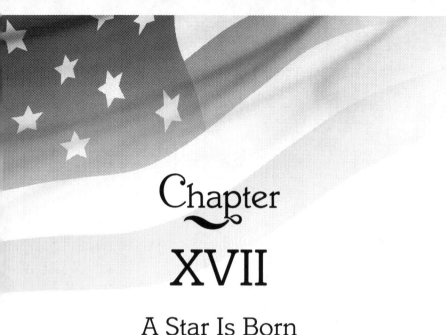

Chapter

XVII

A Star Is Born

The hiring of pooers became a very large and organized endeavor. The pooer employment department was housed in a building that held more than 2,500 Pooville company employees. These were all dooers. Their sole responsibility was to interview and screen potential pooers. Since there was no skill required of the pooers besides eating and pooing, the interviewers were mostly concerned with obtaining individuals who fit the pooer personality profile. The PPP had been developed to identify candidates who wanted to be taken care of financially, with as little effort as possible on their part. Occasionally, a hire would slip through the cracks and become a problem, but for the most part, the new pooers fell in line quickly, and it was easy to find candidates.

One recent hire made by the Pooville company was a male gentleman by the name of Tommy P. Roller. T.P., as he was nicknamed by the pooers, was in his early forties. He was a high school graduate and had worked in the retail clothing industry since he graduated from high school. He lost his job after twenty years of working for the clothing retail company called the Bricks and Mortar Clothing Company. In a downsizing by the company, Mr. Roller was laid off. Bricks and Mortar Clothing Company closed more than one hundred stores as a result of losing business to the trend of online sales. T.P. had been unemployed for several years since being laid off, and his unemployment checks and savings ran out. He had been married to his high school sweetheart, Janie, and they had a twenty-year-old daughter. T.P. and his wife divorced when the money ran out and they lost their home. Tough times had really set into their lives. His wife and daughter moved back to her family's house in New Mexico after the split. T.P. also lost his pension after his pension plan company went bankrupt. T.P. was depressed, broke, and mostly all alone. His so-called friends pretty much labeled him a loser and moved on, leaving him alone. T.P. appeared to be the perfect Pooville pooer profile—almost a perfect 100 percent on his PPP score.

T.P. was hired and moved to Pooville as a pooer. T.P. was very happy that he had landed the pooer position. It was not long before he fell into line and started getting caught up in the pooers' lifestyle. Several months went by, and T.P. started to realize that the mortality rate of the pooers was off the charts. Some of the pooers he was making friends with were disappearing. T.P. was wondering if the pooers' lifestyle could be to blame or if there was something else going on in Pooville. He also noticed that the clinics were really advertised and encouraged by Pooville company management as a place to go if a pooer needed help with their overall health or just aches and pains. He noticed that most pooers had some type of medication prescribed to them, and continuous monitoring resulted in more medications being prescribed. T.P. started to get concerned that maybe there was more going on in Pooville than met the eye.

There was very little day-to-day monitoring of the pooers required by Pooville company management, outside of knowing where they were to deliver prescriptions. Most pooers did not need to be monitored. During the night, pooers were pretty much left to sleep unless they elected to go out and eat and poo. They were exhausted by their strenuous routine of eating and pooing all day long. After a long day filled with eating, pooing, and socializing, the pooers were ready to get a good night's sleep.

Cell phones and computers were permitted in the Pooville area, but few pooers had one or wanted one. Pooville wanted the pooers to feel as though they had the option to either have or not have a cell phone. By forbidding them, Pooville company management felt more of the pooers would want one. Most pooers saw no need to have either a cell phone or a computer. Most of them had abandoned their bank accounts as well as other outside distractions, so they had no way to access funds if they had them. Pooers needed no money because everything was provided for them. Most pooers had no funds. T.P. was an exception to the rule. He had both a cell phone and a laptop computer and was pretty good at using them. He had taught himself pretty good basic computer and cell phone skills.

T.P. started to research what was going on in Pooville regarding the pooers. Why were so many pooers dying? Most prematurely. Why were there so many clinics located in such a small area? How come the pooers never had visitors? Why were there so many pooers getting prescriptions? Especially for opioids. How was this allowed? Why was the government not investigating the situation? T.P. was getting very concerned. His research led him to believe that maybe the lobbies were strong enough and influential enough that the responsible officials within the government who investigated and regulated events like this turned a blind eye to the situation. Years and years of the same congressmen and senators being reelected might have helped to create this situation. Over and over. Term after term for twenty years, thirty years, and in some cases forty years, these congressmen and senators were reelected. Could this be the way the lobbies got to exert the maximum influence over those in a position of power? Could it possibly be that some of our elected officials were beholden to these lobbies? Would all Americans be better off if all elected officials at the local, state, and federal levels were restricted to two terms in office? Would this change help eliminate the immense influence that lobbies held over our elected officials? Would it give our government the opportunity to get new blood and ideas into our legislative system?

T.P. felt it would really help. He knew efforts had been made to make this change in the past without success. Whenever the subject was brought up, it was met with immediate resistance from politicians as well as other influential groups that were interested in keeping the status quo.

T.P. started to hold secret meetings with small groups of the pooers to gather information from them about what was going on in Pooville—what was *really* going on in Pooville. To T.P.'s total astonishment, most of the pooers had no clue what was going on in Pooville. All they knew was that they were taken care of as long as they ate a lot and pooed a lot.

T.P. started to realize just how powerful the Pooville company was and how much influence their lobbying efforts had on decisions being made by our government officials, especially when our elected officials had years and years in office to be influenced. Upon further investigation, T.P. uncovered that there was a network of major corporations, companies, elite families, and private organizations that funneled millions and millions of dollars into these lobbies so that they could enrich themselves at the expense of the vooters, which were basically lower- and middle-class Americans. T.P. discovered that this had been going on for decades in the United States and that it would take a huge effort from the vooters in order to bring about a change to this process. T.P. felt that the only way to save our country was to somehow someway get term limits voted in as the law of the land. He thought it would require a law or an amendment to the Constitution limiting to two terms all elected officials at the local, state, and federal levels but especially at the federal level. After all, two terms was sufficient for our president and vice president. It should also be acceptable for our other elected officials.

T.P. became more and more concerned about the whole situation. These are our elected representatives. We look up to them. It's not possible that they would sell us down the river. T.P. decided to make a list of why the current system was not working and why it was working.

He was confused and did not understand how something like this could be going on for so long. He listed why having politicians reelected term after term after term is a good thing and why it is a bad idea. His reasoning he summarized below:

Pros—why it would not be good to change our current laws regarding term limits:

Long-term congresspeople and senators know their way around Washington and can get to different meetings and conferences without getting lost.

Long-term members already have housing and do not need to waste time finding a place for them and their families to live.

Long-term members have many friends that they can talk to regarding issues that are going to be voted upon.

Long-term members have no problem finding friends and associates who will buy them dinners, vacations, trips, and other perks for them and their families.

Long-term members already have very nice, fully equipped offices with staff members in place. This leads to no disruption in the status quo.

Lobbyists can spend less time and money in their efforts to influence elected officials.

Once influenced, the elites can spend less money in the future to maintain their influence over our elected officials.

Pros—agreements for having term limits for all elected officials:

We would break the grip that lobbies have on our elected officials because two terms would be expensive and would not allow sufficient time for the lobbies to influence our lawmakers.

We would diminish the power and influence that our elites have over our elected officials because elected officials would change every two terms.

It would allow new blood and ideas to continually flow through our government.

It would help reduce the power the political machine has over the politicians.

It would open the door for everyday citizens and nonpoliticians to run for election to public office.

Funding from the elites and the political machine would not be as important to be elected to office.

The political machine of long-term elected officials in their home district or state is so powerful and funded by their parties that lobbies and special interests control their reelection. It is very difficult for a new candidate to run against them. Getting the party's nomination is very difficult if not impossible, creating a monopoly on continuous power.

The lobbies have great influence over many of our representatives on the issues that are important to the companies that they represent, and they spend big bucks to get them reelected at the expense of the vooters who elected them.

Changing elected officials more often helps to weaken the hold that lobbies and special interests have on our elected officials.

Representatives could stop spending their time trying to get reelected and start thinking about the issues our country is facing instead of their own self-interests.

Many representatives have never had a real job and have no clue how the real world works outside of Washington, DC. Being a politician was never intended to be a career by our founding fathers.

End the domination of the machine and lobbies that influence the laws that are passed and enforced.

Bring fresh ideas into the government through a constant turnover of our elected officials.

Allow our elected officials to experience the real world instead of the artificial environment where they are living.

Break the grip that special interests have on our lives and organizations like the food and drug administration. This greed and undue influence hurts the effectiveness of this and other agencies and lines the pockets of big pharma at the vooter's expense.

Two term limits are good enough for our president and vice president why should it not be good enough for all elected officials?

T.P. looked at the pros and cons of term limits. Based on his analysis, he decided that if he could somehow get term limits passed as part of the law of the land, we would all be better off. It did not matter what party affiliation you were; we all would be better off if our elected officials were limited to two terms in office. Period. No exceptions.

Chapter

XVIII

The Times They Are a Changing

Tommy P. Roller put in his resignation and left Pooville after six months of employment. Pooville company management was surprised at his decision because he was a model pooer, and they made every effort to get T.P. to change his mind. They offered him special meals and a semiprivate room and unlimited opioids if he stayed. T.P. was determined to try to help change our country for the better. He saw a very dangerous situation involving a huge section of the Pooville population. T.P felt that being fat, dumb, and happy was not necessarily the right way to live. He basically had nothing but the clothes on his back, and he received no severance pay. The Pooville company made sure that when you came into Pooville as a pooer, you were dependent on Pooville for your survival. T.P. was scared and lonely and had not a clue what was going to happen to him, but he was determined to try to make a difference. He was a driven nonpooer.

T.P. hitchhiked his way to Baltimore, Maryland, which was not too far from the town of Pooville. Baltimore had seen better days, and there were lots of very inexpensive, run-down housing. After sleeping in an alley for a few days, T.P. found a job loading trucks in Baltimore at a warehouse close to the Port of Baltimore for five bucks an hour, cash. It was enough to keep him going until he could figure out how to get his message out on what was going on in our government and how term limits were part of the solution to this problem. T.P was convinced of it.

T.P. spent his free time researching the influence that lobbies had on our government. He wanted to see if the length of time an official spent in office had any effect on their behavior. What were the major industries affected? Who were the players in the government and the names of the major contributors? T.P. was just getting by financially. His cushy life as a pooer was behind him. No more free housing. No more free food. No more free doctor care. No more free prescriptions. No more free education. The green space provided by Pooville was history, but he felt he had a purpose. T.P. was a man driven to make a difference, but how? He had nothing. How could he get his message out to the vooters? He said to himself, "How can a nobody like me overcome all these obstacles and get the law of the land changed?" He knew that the major media outlets, including the TV stations, were owned by media giants and were controlled by the elites and those who supported the Washington lobbies. He knew that the major newspapers were also only going to report what they were told to by their owners, which were also owned by the elites and supported the lobbies. Where could he turn for help? Who would listen to his story? Who would help him change the world? The greatest and most powerful country in the world. How would anyone pay any attention to him?

While working at the loading dock, one of his new friends told him about a publishing company in downtown Baltimore that published financial and social media newsletters to millions of everyday folks throughout the US and all over the world. His friend felt that this organization's goal was to get the true story out to folks in the US as well as all over the world. There were many quality publications that were published by this publishing outlet by some very good individuals. They covered a variety of subjects, including investments, health and social issues, political subjects, and more. He felt it was worth a try to talk to them about his findings if they would talk to him.

T. P. was invited to come to the office and meet with Bret Lawson, one of the principals at the Baltimore office of the Truthful Publishing company, to discuss what he was investigating and what he had found out to date. Although some of the information presented was pretty available and was already fairly well known, no one had pulled together so much information with names, timelines, and events telling a story of tremendous influence by these Washington-based lobbies on government officials, especially when they had served in office for more than two terms. T.P. felt that one of the best ways to restore integrity in government and to once again have elected officials care more for the vooters' issues than being reelected or their own agenda or the lobbies' or special-interest agendas was to somehow get the law changed to limit all elected officials to two terms in office. After all, how could the horrible opioid situation be allowed to continue unabated in our country for so long without the responsible politicians being influenced by the drug industry?

Mr. Lawson discussed T.P.'s findings with his

associates at Truthful, and they liked what T.P. had to say. After consultation and discussions with him, they hired T.P. to work in their research department and to continue putting together his investigation on the term-limits issue. T.P. was so energized by the new employment that his boss had to force him to leave the office and get some rest. Many nights, T.P. would return to the office after hours and work all night putting his investigation together. He was a driven man. He wanted to show everyday Americans as well as the vooters of our country how off track our politicians have gone. He also thought a lot about the pooers. How could he help them see how they were being manipulated by the town of Pooville, the Pooville company, and the elites who ran Pooville?

Over the next several months, a campaign was launched through several Truthful publications and email outlets to make vooters more aware of T.P.'s findings. The effort took place on several fronts and reached millions of Americans. It was heavily published on the internet and was included in many of the paid subscriptions in various newsletters and subscriptions.

There was little if any support from any of the elected officials to change any of the rules regarding the number of terms that they could serve in office. This was a well-paying job with tons of perks and included many ways to make extra money. At this point, both sides of the aisle in Washington were in total gridlock. Nothing was being accomplished, government was in total disarray, and neither side supported the sitting elected president in any of the initiatives that he was trying to advance to make our country a better place to live.

Our enemies were very encouraged at the situation and were making inroads into the destruction of our country. China was especially pleased at what was occurring in the US government. The Chinese could send their brightest students to our elite colleges and universities to be educated. Upon graduation, they would return to China to work for China's stated goal: world domination. This situation had been going on for years and years and had allowed the Chinese to get very competitive with the US, using our own technology and, in some cases, to overtake our dominance. World domination was their stated goal, and nothing was going to stop them. Many of the previous administrations encouraged this situation. This was being done at the exclusion of having some of our American students being educated at these institutions. Self-interest of our elites and politicians was the rule of the day.

The US government was broke and was over $24 trillion in debt, and it was climbing at an alarming rate. The government was in danger of shutting down if the debt ceiling was not raised. Our military was a disaster and in a state of decline. Our leaders squandered billions of dollars on meaningless wars. Our infrastructure was in deplorable condition. Thousands of our bridges were unsafe, and many of our roads were in desperate need of repair. Our airports were a mess. Illegals were flooding over our southern border, and most of our politicians encouraged the situation or did not seem to care. The people coming over the border illegally were to an extent regular folks trying to find a place where they could make a living and support their families, but many others were drug dealers, human traffickers, felons, and the like. Instead of encouraging people to enter the country legally many of the politicians were encouraging the illegals to enter the country any way they could. Many of our politicians were pushing a socialist agenda as the way to solve our problems. Many of our politicians pushing the socialist agenda modeled their programs after the Pooville company's operating model. It worked well for Pooville, so why not expand it to run our country?

Chapter

XIX

Toilet Paper to the Rescue

*A*fter several months of providing information on the situation in Washington in writing and on the web and bringing home the importance of changing the laws of the land to vote in term limits, the vooters in the US started to listen. Vooters from both parties were throwing their support behind the idea in record numbers. Enough was enough. The nonsense going on in Washington had to stop.

Of course, the major TV stations as well as the major newspapers wanted nothing to do with the idea or the story. These companies were owned by the elites and launched a major advertising campaign extolling the importance of having long-term career politicians. The thought of losing any of their grip on the vooters was a hard idea to swallow. The elected officials for the most part were their puppets and wanted nothing to do with this idea. They also would lose their cushy jobs. They could not let that happen. There were a few voices from both parties that thought that this was long overdue, but they were junior officials and were quickly put in their place by the party leaders as well as the elites.

T.P. knew that in order to get this change part of the law of the land, a question would probably need to be included on the national election ballot that was coming up in the next national election. The question could be a simple yes-or-no question of one line. It would read something like this: *Would you support an amendment to the Constitution to have a maximum of two term limits for all elected officials?*

T.P. knew that an amendment to the Constitution would be the only way possible to make it the law of the land. He had no idea how he would be able to accomplish getting this included on the national ballot. This would come about only with a huge effort by the vooters and with the assistance of a powerful political force that thought it was important for the future success of our country.

The term-limit idea reached the White House and was brought to the president's attention by his staff. The sitting president was a very unpopular president with both elected houses. Pretty much everything he was trying to accomplish was being blocked by both sides of the aisle. He had very little time for their nonsense. He had a country to run that had huge problems. He had no time for this petty infighting. The only reason he was in the White House was that his popularity was high among a majority of vooters from both parties. That was it. They liked what he was doing and what he had promised to do once he was elected.

After consultation with his staff, the president decided to support the effort to bring term limits into the federal government. He told the vooters that he would put the full weight of his presidency behind this idea if he was given a total of one million verifiable vooter signatures supporting this idea. He would then consult with his legal advisers to decide the easy way to include this question on the ballot in the national election for the vooters to decide. T.P. fell off his chair when he heard the news.

T.P. remained silent on the floor of his office for more than an hour, with tears streaming down his face. How could an unemployed Pooville pooer who left the company homeless and totally broke and alone be able to, within a six-month period, convince the president of the United States to put his idea on the ballot for the national election? He was stunned, but he concluded that this was the United States of America. The greatest country in the world. Possibly the greatest country of all time. That was how an event like this was possible.

The national media, including the major TV stations and newspapers, again launched a vicious attack to stop this movement in its tracks. The campaign against this idea stressed how important it was to have the most experienced politicians representing us in Congress. The more the media attacked the idea, the more the vooters supported the idea. They could see right through this argument and knew it was a load of poo.

A major countrywide effort was made to collect petitions to present to the president to show how much support there was for this idea. The entire effort was accomplished with volunteers. In less than four weeks, more than five million verifiable signatures supporting the term-limit proposal were collected and presented to the president. He was very impressed and overwhelmed. He was successful in getting this question included on the ballot for the national election.

The election was held the next national election year, and the question was passed by over a 90 percent margin. It was uniformly supported by the electorate from both parties, and a sense of coming together was felt by the vooters of both parties throughout the entire country. The elites as well as the elected officials were livid and vowed to fight to overturn the vote, but that was not going to happen. An amendment to the Constitution was submitted and passed by a two-thirds majority in both the House and the Senate. It was signed by our sitting president and became law. This was the last term that many elected officials throughout the United States would have. The way Washington was going to operate was in for a big change. The vooters were very happy and relieved that the question overwhelmingly passed. They looked forward to taking their government back from the elites and the career politicians who had controlled it for so many years. It was time to return it to the people (vooters). The sitting president was also reelected by a huge margin. A feeling of positive change was sweeping through the land. It was the most positive thing that had happened in American politics for many years. Maybe the days of business as usual were actually coming to an end.

T.P. loved the music of John Lennon. John was his musical idol. His favorite song by John was called "Imagine." T.P. was so moved and astounded by the outcome of the national election that he rewrote John's song "Imagine," reflecting how he felt about the future possibilities for the country. His updated version is below:

Imagine
(government version)

Imagine there's no career politicians.
It's easy if you try.
No lobbies to influence our elected officials,
Below us only good infrastructure.

Imagine all the people
Living for today (ha, ha, ha).

Imagine there are no drug overdoses.
It isn't hard to do.
No prescription drugs that will kill you
And no opioid deaths too.
Imagine all our politicians
Working together to solve the country's
problems.

You may say that I'm a dreamer,
But I'm not the only one.
I hope someday you'll join us
And our country will be as one.

Imagine no huge federal deficit.
I wonder if you can.
No need for our bloated federal government
Or unnecessary regulations too.

Imagine all the people
Sharing all the world.

You may say that I'm a dreamer,
But I'm not the only one.
I hope someday you'll join us
And our country will live as one.

Chapter

XX

T.P. Returns to Pooville

Now that T.P. had been successful in getting the term–limit legislation passed, he was full of confidence that he could change other things in the world that needed attention. What other major issues could he address? His mind wandered back to Pooville and specifically to the situation with the pooers. These were a content group of folks, but T.P. felt that they were being exploited. He did not know fully what was happening to the pooers, but he had a feeling that more was going on in Pooville than met the eye. Something smelled in Pooville.

T.P. discussed the experience that he had in Pooville with his boss at the Truthful Publishing company. He laid out the entire situation as he saw it, including the excessive number of pain clinics in Pooville, the excessive overdoses by the pooers, and the fact that pooers were nearly all obese and died prematurely. T.P. could not put his finger on it, but it just seemed that there was something going on with the pooers in Pooville that didn't smell right. He discussed with Mr. Lawson, his boss, the possibility of changing his name and appearance and applying again for a pooer position in Pooville. T.P. knew exactly what the Pooville company was looking for in a pooer, and he figured he could tailor his new identity to fit the Pooville company requirements exactly. This would allow him to go undercover to try to discover what in the world was going on in Pooville.

Upon lengthy discussions with the Truthful Publishing committee, it was decided to give T.P. a shot at the assignment and figure out a way to get T.P. Roller back into the pooer community with a new identity and a somewhat altered appearance. His new appearance was already partially there because when he left Pooville, he was overweight and shabby. It would be hard to recognize him as the same person now. He had lost fifty pounds. His beard and mustache were gone, and his new haircut was very now. That alone was a big change. His new assignment was to try to figure out exactly what was going on in the pooer community and to determine just how much the Pooville company was involved.

T.P. applied for and was hired under the assumed name of William E. Roll Jr.—Willie Roll, as he was nick named by the pooers. He was very quickly accepted by the pooer community. Willie fit right in. Many of the pooers that Willie had known when he was last in Pooville were no longer around. Willie was amazed at the number of pooers who had passed on since he left. It had only been little more than five years since he left. Willie Roll was very surprised. He was bound and determined to find out what was going on in Pooville.

Willie got quickly absorbed back into the eating and pooing routine. He started to make friends throughout the pooer community and wasted no time in gaining the trust of as many pooers as possible. Early on, he complained of a pain in his neck and was prescribed a liberal dosage of opioids to alleviate the pain. The doctor told him to do less and to sit on his ass more to help alleviate the pain. A new supply of pills was delivered to him every Wednesday like clockwork. Willie just stashed them away. There was no doubt in Willie's mind that these were nothing more than pill mills set up by management to control the pooers.

Willie Roll could keep his cell phone, which happened to be a top-of-the-line Apple iPhone.

Having the phone allowed Willie to send information back to Truthful Publishing on a regular basis. Pooville company management did not pay much attention to the cell phone because pooers had no ability to continue to pay for their phone service or manage a cell phone or internet account. It was never an issue. Willie had kept a very low profile on his cell phone usage for Pooville in the past, and they had no reason to believe they would have any trouble with this policy now. Pooville management never gave it another thought.

Willie was pulled into the main office early on in his pooer employment concerning his pooing activity. He was told his poo quantity was below average, and he either needed to eat more and poo more or he would be terminated for lack of poo. He was put on pooing probation for three months and was told that unless he got his pooing activity up to at least the minimum standard, he would be terminated. Willie was trying to eat as little as possible. He was now a little overweight but generally in good shape; he realized he would really need to pick up the eating and pooing, or he was out of here. Willie started to eat like a man going to the electric chair. It was not long before he was taken off pooing probation.

Willie Roll launched into his investigation by first talking to as many pooers as possible. Willie sought out the pooer hierarchy. These were the shakers and movers of the pooer community. These were the former pooers who had made names for themselves in the annual pooer competition. "How long have you been a pooer?" he would ask them. He asked if any of them had seen or heard anything regarding Pooville procedures. Little by little, Willie started piecing together a deliberate attempt by Pooville company management to addict as many pooers as possible to opioids. Willie could not figure out why it looked like the Pooville company wanted pooers to die. He did not know that this allowed them to have an organized and continuous flow of deceased pooers, which they would harvest to support production of the products dependent on dead pooers. Willie noticed that the dosage of the pills he was receiving was ever so slowly being increased. Why was this going on?

The winner of the Pooville pooing contest this year was a fellow nicknamed Pooee. He was an enormously popular pooer, and this was his second year in a row winning the pooing contest. A rare feat indeed. Poo Bear, you might remember, was the first pooer to win back-to-back pooing contests. Pooee was very well respected by the pooing community because of the large quantity of poo that he created daily. He was the envy of the other pooers. He never went into the pooer community without his poo hat and poo shirt. He was the most popular pooer in Pooville. The other pooers were always asking him for autographs. Fame has no bounds. The dooer management recognized this and gave him more recognition than normal. They wanted to keep him happy. Being the second two-time winner of the pooing contest, Pooville company management announced that a statue of Pooee would be erected on a pedestal right next to Poo Bear in the green area. What an honor. Two revered pooers.

Willie tried to get close to Pooee by sitting at his table, trying to poo in a stall close to his, and so on. He wanted to talk to him. Within a few weeks, they became friends and started to hang out together. Willie started to slowly have conversations with Pooee about the pooer community and what he perceived as potential problems in Pooville.

Pooee organized a secret meeting of the surviving winners of the past pooing contests, as well as many of the runners-up and other great pooers as he could find. These were the hierarchy within the pooer community. If anyone knew what was going on, this group would know. Some of these pooers were only a poo away from becoming the Grand Poopa.

They met in Pooee's private room that was attached but separate from his pooer dormitory. All the who's who of the pooer community, including Poo Bear (he was on his last legs), Pootine (the winner with the all-time record for total poo weight), and Instant Poo, a very colorful fellow who had also seen better days, were there. Many of the others, twenty in all, were some of the elite pooers in Pooville. You might say they were the elites of the pooer community.

Pooee introduced Willie Roll and told the group a little bit about his concerns. Willie outlined some of his concerns about the pooers and asked for their input. The feedback from the group reinforced what Willie was trying to find out. One of the pooers present mentioned that he had heard a rumor that dead pooer bodies were somehow being used in products produced by the Pooville company. The pooer dismissed it, but that would certainly answer the question of motivation for Pooville company management wanting to do in pooers. They talked until the wee hours of the morning and closed the meeting by heading off to an all-night cafeteria to get a snack before they retired.

The pooers at the meeting mentioned that there was a very elite group of pooers in Pooville known as the smelly pooers. They were elevated by Pooville to special status. The important thing about this elite group of pooers was that they pooed a very special very high-quality poo. It allowed the Pooville company to manufacture a premium quality of their fertilizer that could be sold at a much higher price.

These pooers had their own poo rooms with their names posted on them. They also had semiprivate housing as well as sex privileges and other special perks. One of these pooers was known as Yummy Poo. She was very well known and respected and seemed to be plugged into the Pooville activities. You always knew when Yummy pooed because her poo could be smelled for about a mile from her poo room. The other pooers would always comment, "Yummy just pooed. I think it's yummy." She was very popular. The pooer committee at the meeting suggested that Willie should contact Yummy Poo to discuss further what he was trying to find out. Pooee, who was very good friends with Yummy Poo, introduced Willie to her.

Chapter

XXI

The Plot Exposed

Willie and Yummy immediately hit it off. She told Willie that there was something going on in Pooville, but she could not put her finger on what exactly it was. She mentioned the cold storage facilities that were scattered throughout Pooville. Why were there so many? Why were they so big? Many questions with no answers. They decided that they would try to have a look into one of them to see what was going on. Yummy, Willie, and a few of the other pooers on the committee met close to one of the cold rooms after dark in order to get a good, uninterrupted look inside. These facilities were not even locked. The dooers were so sure that the pooers didn't care a poo about what happened to

125

them that they did not even bother to lock the place.

When they went inside, they were shocked to find dead pooers hanging on hooks all over the cold room. It looked like a slaughterhouse for livestock. The dead pooers were naked and hanging in rows. They had been gutted, and it looked like their internal organs had been removed. The pooers at first just stood there in disbelief. They started to recognize some of them. They all went into shock. Yummy started to cry. They all stood there in silence, just staring. Very little was said. There were hundreds housed in the room. They all looked very white because the blood had been drained from them. As they were examining the room, they did not realize that this was just the first step in the manufacturing process of Pooville fertilizer products. Before leaving, Willie took many pictures with his iPhone, documenting the situation in the cold room.

They left the cold room without saying much to one another. Before they disbanded, they all decided that they would meet the next night and try to find out what happened to the dead pooers after they were removed from the cold storage room. The following night, the pooers all met near another cold room that saw a lot more activity. A lot of the dooers were always coming and going. A lot was going on in this building. Again, the building was left unlocked. They went in at night, and again no one was there when they entered. Dead pooers were located all over this building. They were in the process of being dismembered. There were huge carts containing heads in one, arms and legs in another, torsos in another. It was very gruesome but very well organized. Several from the pooer committee were crying and immediately left the cold room. Several others just stood and stared. Willie knew he had finally figured out what was going on. He immediately started to photograph the room, with as much detail as he could capture with his iPhone.

There were banks of huge grinders located in the center of the cold room, with huge hoppers on top of them. You could tell that the body parts moved toward the grinders. It was for sure that this was the pooers' final destination in this room. Willie again photo documented the situation.

The pooer committee led by Willie decided to meet the next night to see what the next step in the investigation should be. The following day, Willie Roll snooped around to try to figure out where they should go next.

There was a huge building next to the building that dissected the body parts. That looked like the next logical step in the process, and he was right.

Willie also noticed that there were identical building configurations scattered throughout Pooville.

The next night as they approached the next building, they quickly realized that the building was occupied, and it looked like it was producing a variety of end products. They could see that many pallets were loaded with bags of fertilizer, and other products were stacked up in various places. Willie got a few photos of the place without being noticed, but they decided to come back Sunday night when maybe nobody would be working. When the pooer committee returned on Sunday night, sure enough, the place was empty. Willie and his crew got a good look inside, and it was obvious what happened to the dead pooers and how they were processed into Pooville company products.

The next night, the entire committee met in Yummy Poo's room and reviewed the photos as well as their other findings. At the meeting, Willie disclosed to them that he was working undercover for a major publishing company. and his mission was to uncover what was going on in Pooville regarding the pooers. Why were so many pooers prematurely dying? And why were so many opioids being distributed to pooers in unusually large quantities? The committee applauded Willie Roll's efforts and told him they would cooperate in any way possible to help him get his story told.

Willie made sure that the committee knew how important secrecy was in the investigation. The Pooville company could not be given any time to react to the allegations that would be brought against them.

At this point, Willie Roll informed his boss that he thought he had the information he was seeking and it would be prudent for him to resign and go back to Baltimore. Truthful Publishing agreed, and Willie gave his notice and returned to his headquarters. The Pooville company tried to discourage Willie Roll from leaving, but Willie told them he was just getting too fat and had to leave. The Pooville company did not know that any investigations were going on involving them. T.P. Rollers was very grateful that he had been given the assignment to solve the mystery, and he was especially glad to get the hell out of Pooville. Since the home office had downloaded the entire contents of his iPhone, he left it with Yummy Poo in case they needed any additional information in their investigation. Willie was very happy that he was out of Pooville—and this time for good.

Chapter

XXII

The Story of Pooville

W hen T.P. Roller got back to Truthful Publishing, he was treated like a hero. His salary was immediately doubled. Management had a huge coming-home party in his honor. They knew that they had the story of the century, and what T.P. had uncovered was nothing short of spectacular. This was a company that was the envy of the world. The town of Pooville and the Pooville company were so secretive that no information had ever gotten beyond their walls. T.P. had penetrated the inner workings of the Pooville company. His investigation blew the lid off the Pooville company. This was a story that had to be told, and Truthful Publishing had the media and other resources necessary to get it to the people.

T.P. was invited to join the writing staff of the very talented crew of Truthful writers, editors, and so on. It took several months to put the story together. There were quite a few times that T.P. had to contact Yummy Poo to gather additional details. They knew they had to get the facts right. The Pooville company was very powerful, rich, and well connected. They had many friends in high places. Truthful knew that Pooville would push back with everything they had. It was very important to get this right. The story of Pooville just had to be told.

Truthful Publications published more than thirty publications, covering finance, politics, health issues, investing, travel, and more. They had an audience of millions of readers located in the US, Europe, and throughout the world. They reached their audience through the distribution of weekly, monthly, and quarterly newsletters. Some of these publications were owned by Truthful, but the vast majority were independently owned. Truthful did the printing, distribution, and administrative and collection requirements of publishing a newsletter for many of their clients.

Truthful, in an unusual move, asked their newsletter principals to come to their headquarters for an important meeting. Every newsletter was represented at the meeting. Before disclosing their report and findings, each representative signed a secrecy agreement not to disclose any information prior to publication. In the meeting, Truthful outlined their findings regarding the investigation of the Pooville company. After the presentation, they asked every publication to put aside their normal newsletter format and for one time only to join them in sending out the findings on the Pooville company. They felt this was so important that if every newsletter agreed, the bombshell they were looking for would surely drop. After much discussion and a little arm twisting by Truthful, every publication agreed to publish the same report regarding the Pooville company. T.P. Roller gave a special speech at the end of the meeting, laying out his role in the investigation. This was very instrumentational in getting agreement from all newsletters.

Four months after T.P. returned from Pooville, the reports were released to the public. Every newsletter publication was released on the same day to obtain the maximum effect. The articles were all titled "The Story of Pooville."

Some were delivered via the internet, and some were mailed reports. Almost immediately, there was a firestorm of media coverage. Within two weeks, every major television network was reporting on the goings-on in Pooville. The state and federal government sent every agency that could possibly have any involvement into Pooville. This of course included the Maryland State Police, the FBI, and many other local, state, and federal agencies. The president instructed both houses of Congress to immediately launch investigations into the allegations. Both the town of Pooville and the Pooville company were scrambling to try to cover up what they had been doing. The repercussions were so swift that Pooville had no time to react.

When the story of Pooville was released, the result was the total shutdown of the Pooville company. This was a company that produced more than 90 percent of the world's fertilizer and related products. They were basically a monopoly in the fertilizer business. They shipped billions and billions of dollars of their products all over the world. The Pooville company was listed in the top one hundred companies in the US and was one of the most profitable companies on earth. This was a big deal.

The raids by various agencies resulted in almost a thousand arrests. Pauly Poo and most of the Poo family who were involved in the company, as well as the board of directors, were arrested. Many of the dooers were also arrested. More than three hundred pain clinics were closed as a result of the investigation. Mass arrests of drug manufacturers and distributors were made. This was long overdue. The infractions by the drug manufacturers and distributors were so blatant that even several middle-level department heads were arrested and charged with crimes. In a very short period, the town of Pooville fell into ruins, and the Pooville company filed for bankruptcy.

Pooville's ultimate downfall was their underestimation of the pooer community. Pooville's elites had no respect for the pooers. They thought that they had reduced them to possessions, that they could control and handle them as they pleased. By being so lax in their thinking, they opened the door for the pooers to unravel what was happening to them in Pooville and cause their downfall.

Chapter

XXIII

The Rise of the Pooers

The poor pooers did not fully realize what was going on in Pooville. After the dust settled, the heads of the various agencies assembled the pooers and told them what had been going on. Many of them were crying and deeply saddened by what had happened to their friends and fellow pooers. Since the US government proclaimed that the Pooville company was a criminal enterprise, the government was able to confiscate a large section of the town of Pooville as well as most of the assets of the Pooville company. In an effort to compensate the pooers for years of service and to try to recover some sense of order to the town of Pooville and the Pooville company, by executive order, the president of the United States ordered that a new company be formed. Shares of the new company that were voting common stock were to be issued to each dooer, based on their length of service to the Pooville Fertilizer Company. The rest would be sold via an IPO (initial public offering) after the new company was formed and operational. The pooer population represented more than 50 percent of Pooville's population. They renamed the town Pooersville and renamed the company the Pooersville Fertilizer Company. The pooers now found themselves being part owners in a new company, and they would have their say in its operation. Many of the pooers sold their shares in the company once the company went public and the lock-up period ended. Some of the other pooers continued to buy shares of the company and became major shareholders. Of course, it was their choice.

One of the first orders of business was to honor the dead pooers that were being held in cold storage and to give them a proper funeral. At the same time, they needed to address the massive opioid-addiction problems they had in the pooer population. There were a lot of hurting pooers, and opioids were no longer available. A committee of the pooers was formed. They brought in many doctors and therapists and used the old clinic buildings to create rehab operations. Slowly but surely, they rehabilitated the majority of the pooer population. There were some failures, but for the most part, the pooers kicked the habit and got back to the business of pooing.

The pooers reunited in a common goal of carving out a new life for themselves. Many of them ran for different offices when they held elections, and some were elected and established a hierarchy of management. Several of the well-known pooers were elected to high positions. This included Poo Bear, who was elected president of the company. Yummy Poo was elected vice president in charge of production and product development. Some of the other well-known pooers were elected to important positions. The new company slowly began to emerge and take shape as the Pooersville Fertilizer Company. Their common goal was to get fertilizer production up and running again. They ceased production of all Pooville enhancers because of what was used in them, but the fertilizer was still the biggest seller. This product alone could sustain the pooers' new company until they came up with some new products.

The pooers were a determined bunch and promised to poo more than they did before (hard to believe) in an effort to grow the company.

Over time, new housing was constructed for all pooers. A lottery system determined the order that the new housing was assigned. Each high-rise building consisted of one-, two- and three-bedroom units. Many of the pooers preferred to live with one or two of their close friends instead of living alone. Marriage and other normal arrangements were allowed. This new system would accommodate everyone's wishes. Each unit included private sleeping areas and a living room and small kitchenette. There were no bathrooms in any unit, but the first floor of each building was taken up by a pooatorium that accommodated fully automated pooing activities. Most of the existing pooatoriums were modified to make them more comfortable, and the very old ones were torn down and replaced with modern, updated facilities.

There were many dooers who were still living in Pooville after the arrests. A lot of them had no idea what had been going on with the pooers. If a dooer had not been involved in the manufacturing process, they probably had not been aware of what was going on. There was a strict policy of secrecy, so many of the dooers had not been aware of the manufacturing process.

The pooers and dooers came together in the common goal of resurrecting the new Pooersville company. They knew they could sell all the product they could produce. Demand was strong. Within a year, they were shipping a consistent supply of

Pooersville fertilizer. They were only at 30 percent of the previous production levels, but they were climbing as they became more and more organized. Many of the dooers were given very good positions in the new company.

The pooers started to receive weekly paychecks for their efforts. Some of the profits that the company realized were distributed as dividends to stockholders, but the majority of the profits were plowed back into the company to support the tremendous growth they were experiencing. Stock prices were rising.

Winnie Poo was elected to head up production and new product development. This was one pooer who had a head on her shoulders. Winnie was also rated as a magic smelly pooer. She, like Yummy Poo, had very special poo—smelly but full of special potent ingredients not found in most pooers' poo. She was very well respected in the pooer community because of her poo and business prowess.

The first thing Winnie did after taking office was go on a mission to locate the dooers who worked in the R&D department of the former Pooville company. Many of the dooers who worked there were arrested because of their involvement in manipulating the death of pooers, but many of them were not involved and did not even realize that this was happening. Winnie managed to find the bulk of them and rehired many of them as Pooersville company employees.

In their first meeting, the dooers told Winnie that they were working on a very exciting new product line, and it was in the late stages of development. Unknown to the pooer population, the Pooville company had been working on a method to turn the pooers' pee into an exciting new energy drink. They were also experimenting with a super energy tonic and a line of soft drinks that tasted a lot better and were much better for you than a lot of the sodas currently available on the market. This was exciting news. Up until this point, pee had been a waste by-product in Pooville. To harvest and create new products based on pee would create a whole new profit stream in Pooersville.

Within a year, the R&D department under Winnie's leadership was able to get three new products approved, launched, and into production. The demand shot through the roof for these products, and they eventually became a larger product line than Pooersville natural fertilizer.

A new group of Pooersville positions opened for peeers. If you could really pee up a storm, the Pooersville company wanted you, and they were willing to offer a signing bonus for coming on board. Legends like PP, Pee Pee La Pee, Pee Pee

Power, Fire Hose, and Patty Pee were all eventually honored in Pooersville. Of course, I could go on and on about famous peeers and all the excitement surrounding their lives, but it would take too long. Maybe for another time or my next exciting book.

Over the next ten years, the Pooersville Fertilizer Company shipped more fertilizer than when the Poo family controlled it. The product was 10 percent less expensive but was even better because it really was a natural product.

Additionally, the Pooersville all-natural energy and soft drink line took substantial market share away from the existing products available. The very distinguished nutty flavor was very popular. It was a real hit with both young and old alike.

Chapter

XXIV

I Want to Change the World

T wenty years had passed since term limits were made the law of the land. With the passing of the term-limit amendment legislation, the entire makeup of Congress pretty much changed. Gone were the career politicians. Gone were the elected officials who had been elected for twenty years, thirty years, and even forty years. Being in politics was no longer considered a career. The candidates running for office were not primarily lawyers. There were businessmen, teachers, airline pilots, doctors, contractors, programmers, dooers, pooers, peeers, entrepreneurs, and more. The big budgets needed to elect a lot of these folks were gone because the elites could no longer keep them in office for long enough to control the way they voted.

The lobbies were on their last legs. Incoming funds supporting various causes and legislation were drying up. No longer could an elected official be kept in office for years and years. The entire makeup of the House and Senate was changing. The egress of lobbyists was so severe that the high-priced real estate market in the Washington, DC, area was dropping in value. Property values were depressed due to the departure of so many fat cats and lobbyists leaving Washington. After all, who would ever want to live in Washington, DC, if they did not have to?

The gridlock was changing at a tremendous pace. Both houses were reaching across the aisle to each other to solve problems instead of trying to grind government to a halt. There was progress on all fronts to make our country a better place to live. Gone were the days of being controlled by special interests. The vooters were what mattered. The president was brought into the conversation and was there to help solve the issues of the day. God bless America.

When the term-limit legislation passed in the US, the country was in a horrible condition. Our national dept was out of control, our military was weak and getting weaker, China was stealing our technology at an alarming rate, and our TV and newspapers were owned and had been corrupted by the elites in an effort to try to sway the vooters to support their own selfish goals. Our infrastructure was in deplorable condition. The federal government had wasted money over the previous twenty years to support foolish wars and other pork barrel projects and special-interest spending programs left the country broke. We were on the verge of collapse.

A program was voted into law to reduce our massive national dept to zero over a twenty-five-year period.

The most difficult spending issues were addressed and solved through mutual respect from both parties. Gone were the days that being reelected was the most important issue that an elected official had to deal with.

The first election after the term-limit law went into effect was a midterm election, and more than half of the House and Senate seats were vacant. The rest were one-term candidates who were fighting for reelection. The country and especially the vooters seemed energized by this new opportunity presented to them. The mood of the country was changing. A new structure was forming of elected officials who were more concerned about solving the problems that our country needed to address rather than politics and being reelected. Both houses came together in the common cause of trying to get back the superpower status the United States once had.

Other issues that were addressed included an overhaul of our immigration system and the completion of security issues involving our southern border, a huge reduction in government spending by closing ineffective departments, reducing needless and expensive regulations, streamlining and updating our antiquated internal government computer systems, and more. A renaissance took place in our country that allowed us to once again obtain the GDP growth of yesteryear. Real wages were increasing, and real prosperity was returning to the United States of America.

Job creation was happening everywhere. Instead of companies leaving the United States, a number of new bills were introduced and passed by both houses that offered incentives to companies that created jobs right here in the good old USA. Gone was the idea of exporting our jobs to other countries. Many industries that were previously left for dead came roaring back. We were once again the envy of the world.

At this point, the Pooersville company and the town of Pooersville were thriving. The new transparency that the pooers created in all their activities served to create a model city and company for other American companies to follow. Gone were the walls, fences, and gates. Transparency was the issue of the day.

Many of the peeers and pooers became national celebrities. Pooersville had guided tours of their facility and pointed out where some of the legendary pooers and peeers lived. There were many statues situated throughout the town of Pooersville featuring famous pooers and peeers who had passed away.

One of the great national events that took place each year immediately after the Super Bowl was the peeer versus pooer contest. It was very exciting, had ratings sometimes higher than the Super Bowl, and featured the best pooers and peeers that Pooersville had to offer competing against one another.

Prosperity once again return to our beloved country. God bless the United States of America.

I'd love to change the world,
But I don't know what to do,
So I'll leave it up to you.

—Lyrics by Ten Years After

Printed in the United States
by Baker & Taylor Publisher Services